The Miranda Revolution

Can a mother's love bring down a brutal dictatorship?

First published by Createspace in 2015

This edition 2019

© Derek McMillan

The Archbishop's Torturer

The Prince-Archbishop Wolf-Dietrich Von Raitenau, undisputed ruler of Salzburg, was renowned for having the most cost-efficient of torturers. The young man's name was Xavier Hollands. He claimed privately to have known the Prince-Archbishop in what he insisted on calling "a parallel universe." Wolf-Dietrich, whom Xavier addressed in private as "Wolfie", forgave his torturer this eccentricity because he really was very very good.

Unusually for someone in his profession, Xavier had an aversion to actually torturing people. However, prisoners of the Prince-Archbishop soon found out that a conversation with Xavier would elicit any information his torturee might possess. There was no point in lying to him or remaining silent. The rumour that he had supernatural powers spread in Salzburg and he found that this made his job easier. Naturally enough nobody reported him to the civil or religious authorities for witchcraft for the simple reason that the civil and religious authorities answered to the Prince-Archbishop, his employer.

Wolfie could never quite be sure whether Xavier was really an angel or a devil. He was supremely confident that he could deal with either. Xavier did not have a room in the castle and he cultivated the rumour that he never slept. Like many things Xavier says this could be taken with a pinch of salt. Fortunately Salzburg has a plentiful supply.

Back, or perhaps we should say forwards, in the twenty-first century Xavier made a discovery, or as his wife Tilly has it "stumbled upon" how to make a hard astral projection. The full implications of this only became clear to him during the first Salt War. The practical upshot of this was that far from never sleeping, he could be said to be sleeping on the job 24/7.

Xavier, the "real" Xavier, was quite safe in a carefully sealed room "somewhere in London." Many of his waking hours were spent frequenting Ye Olde Boar.

The best of pies

Kaspar, a newcomer, was holding forth at Xavier's table in Ye Olde Boar. "It was the best of pies. It was the worst of pies. I have to admit the pastry could not be faulted. I actually enjoyed it. Then as soon as I bit into the pie I found that it was all gristle and bits of animal I prefer not to speculate about."

There were several sympathetic noises around the table as Kaspar continued, "The Commanding Officer stood over me and made sure I ate every scrap of it too. I noticed that all of the troops who were going out to the forward base ate these pies. It was as if it were some kind of toughening-up exercise.

"I was there," (*I should mention that Kaspar was a journalist formerly employed by The Dictator*) "to report on the victory over the hill tribes who had been revolting. The Dictator was going to defeat them in the next four days. If there were no victory there would be no report. The CO cheerily told me not to worry about it because in that case I would probably be dead anyway. He actually slapped me on the back quite hard and the officers who were sitting at the table with me found it quite amusing.

"Orders were shouted and echoed around this dreadful underground bunker where we had been eating. As we were leaving a subaltern pointed out the steel doors to me.

"'They will hold out for a good four days.' was his confident prediction. If I had any trepidation about the food at the forward base, it was immediately dispelled at my next meal. The food was plentiful and better than I have ever tasted at any army base. The men visibly perked up. Life at the forward base might be a little fraught. Correction, it **was** fraught, what with snipers and improvised explosive devices going off every five minutes. However the food and the conditions were excellent. Nothing like the horror pie of my first night came my way again.

"It was on the second day that the hill tribesmen launched an assault on the camp. I have seen better attacks mounted by unarmed Boy Scouts to be honest with you but the CO gave the order "panic stations" and the men retreated in disorder.

"The soldiers held on to their guns for the most part but I noticed that they dropped their packs in order to move the faster. The disciplined troops looked like a complete and utter rabble. I expected the CO to be incandescent with rage. On the contrary I caught sight of him smiling at the panic. The hill tribesmen were so busy looting the abundant supplies in the camp that they were slow to give chase and the steel doors of the underground redoubt clanged behind us.

"The CO did a piece to camera for me. 'We have just fought a decisive engagement with the rebels and they will give us no trouble for many years to come. The casualties among the hill tribesmen have been catastrophic while as you can see,' (a quick pan around the room) 'all of my men are unharmed.'

"I was baffled. The CO went back to his office with senior officers and a bottle of Scotch. For the rest of us it was the ghastly pies again. To my surprise I saw a number of pies being taken into the CO's office as well.

"Four days later when the steel doors opened again, the hills were eerily silent except for the sound of carrion crows. The forward base and two villages I visited were littered with remains. None of the rebels or their wives and children had a mark on them but it was clear that they had died in agony.

"'Poison?' I asked somewhat incredulously, 'our supplies were all poisoned? So we were eating poison the whole time?'

The CO just nodded.

"'And the pies?' I asked.

The CO told me that I needed to eat one every four days or so. They were vile so that any which fell into the wrong hands were unlikely to be eaten but they did contain the antidote.

The poison takes roughly four days to work as I could see. I was allowed to report the victory but there were to be no details of how it was achieved, just in case we decided to use this method again. It is the Dictator's own idea of course. He is a strong man."

There was a silence around the table after that. We were used to Xavier's tall tales but Kaspar's story had the ring of truth about it.

Eventually Xavier broke the silence.

"So what brings you here?"

Kaspar looked down at his hands. "Working for The Dictator," he began as if to himself. Then he paused. Eventually he continued, "Well it was not a safe occupation. Like I said, he was a strong man, is a strong man. You have heard the story about his children?"

We had all heard rumours and hints about this story but Kaspar seemed to speak with authority.

"His son and heir and his two daughters were kidnapped by a government driver," Xavier prompted.

Kaspar looked at Xavier in surprise and then he continued, "The driver demanded the release of three opposition leaders. The Dictator had the opposition leaders in question brought from prison and the three of them were executed live on TV. This sealed the fate of all the Dictator's living children. Since then he has had many consorts. The consorts are all as alike as plastic surgery can make them and there are rumours of many children."

"And the children he does not want as heirs?" Xavier asked quietly. Kaspar looked at him.

"You know?"

Xavier has never admitted to NOT knowing anything in my hearing so he just let Kaspar continue.

"As far as we know they are taken away and terminated with extreme prejudice. And that brings me to the reason I am in exile. You see, I talked to one of the men responsible for carrying out those orders. As soon as I had that information I realised that it was time for me to get out if I could. Millions can't afford to just walk away from this situation of course.

There were murmurs of sympathy around the table but I noticed that Xavier's eyes were hard. Sometimes I almost believed his tall tale about being a torturer for an archbishop.

"The Dictator has no name. His father did but nobody was ever permitted to use it. He made sure his son was only ever called "The Dictator's son" There was no question of his daughters being allowed to inherit and no question of more than one son surviving. The people live in poverty and the gangsters have taken over all the public services.

Xavier and Kaspar talked long into the night. Several bottles later, for Kaspar had a capacity for red wine to match Xavier's, they had decided on a course of action.

I thought this was just another of those "the revolution starts when this pub closes" discussions. I have heard many of them in Ye Olde Boar. I was in fact quite wrong.

The Mirror of Eternity

It is not possible to travel in time – except one day forwards per day I suppose. What Xavier had developed was called "The Mirror of Eternity" which enabled him to observe events in the past, present and future with the aid of some frankly rather dangerous drugs.

Xavier was lying on his bed playing "good toes, naughty toes" with various parts of his anatomy while we waited for the drugs to have effect. Tilly and I had originally thought that the Mirror of Eternity was just another one of Xavier's tall tales until we had first-hand experience of it. Tilly has also had experience of Xavier's hard astral projection and he never tires of reminding her about it.

Kaspar had more reason than we did to be a little sceptical, either that it would work or that it would help him to find out more verifiable facts about The Dictator. Xavier ushered us in to the sealed room which housed the massive screen of the Mirror of Eternity. I noticed that Kaspar looked askance at the pentacle on the floor which the seats almost completely failed to conceal. This evidence of dark forces did not increase Xavier's credibility in his eyes but he settled back to see what would happen.

Neeta and Petra

We saw a man, Kaspar whispered that it was The Dictator but a few years younger than he remembered him, Xavier quietly told him there was no need to whisper. Nobody could see or hear us. The Dictator appeared to be playing with two young girls, identical twins. By sight they were hard to tell apart but their voices were quite different.

He called them Neeta and Petra. The game seemed quite violent for the kindergarten.

Petra was holding aloft a soft toy.

"Get the bunny, Neeta. Go on!" The Dictator urged

"I've got it, bitch-face!" shouted Petra

Neeta fought fiercely to regain the toy, leaving tracks of blood on Petra's face and arms with her fingernails and all the time screaming the language of the gutter.

The Dictator watched calmly as their training carried on

Eventually little Neeta punched Petra really hard in the stomach and grabbed the toy from her. We watched as she proceeded to tear bunny apart with her strong bare hands.

"What do you want to do now?" The Dictator was rarely shown smiling in public but he certainly smiled sweetly when both girls yelled in unison, "Blow up Teddy!"

The girls tied fireworks to a huge expensive teddy bear.

Petra even ripped into the stuffing to bury a thunderflash in there. The girls squealed with delight as the fireworks tore Teddy apart.

Xavier used the "points of interest" app on his smartphone to take us forward in time to another encounter when young teenagers Petra and Neeta were in training. They were crawling in the mud under barbed wire. When one of them accidentally touched the wire she screamed in pain. The wire was apparently electrified.

We heard Neeta whisper, "Daddy" as she made an effort to gain the few seconds' advantage to allow her to draw level with Petra. Petra started to giggle uncontrollably and Neeta easily finished first. She stood with a smug expression watching her sister struggling in the mud.

Petra shouted at Neeta when she eventually finished the course.

"You bloody bitch!"

She lunged towards Neeta and pulled her hair. Neeta scratched at her face. The uniformed supervisors had to pull the two furious muddy girls apart. Then astonishingly we watched as the girls cuddled and commiserated spreading the mud still further over their clothes if that were possible.

"Oh you poor thing. Look at those scratches. Let me kiss it better for you."

They went off arm in arm to change.

From the diary of Kaspar

I managed to make contact with Xavier Hollands easily enough. He is not secretive at all. Indeed he is so boastful that getting an invitation to see the Mirror of Eternity was child's play. The information about Neeta and Petra was interesting and as far as I could see it was accurate. I can imagine how useful the Mirror of Eternity could be for the Dictator. We thought it might be a myth but it seems that it really works.

As for the "hard astral projection" I have no evidence of that and the whole idea seems to wander into the realms of black magic rather than science. I fail to see how an astral projection (if there is such a thing) can interact with the real world as Xavier claims. However I can see all sorts of possibilities if it does work.

Death to the Dictator!

Xavier's app took us to a house. There was no sign of Neeta and Petra. The blinds were closed against the night and against prying eyes. We found out the names of the four men (there were no women) from the conversation. Kaspar was insistent that they were unlikely to be their real names but it is better than calling them Man1, Man2 etc.

Ygael, a man in his forties perhaps, beginning to grey around the temples, was talking.

"Well I was expecting a rather better turnout than this. I think we should wait another five minutes at least. There was one contact who seemed interested and she is not here yet."

"OK give her a chance." Garcia was quite keen on the idea.

"Garcia always wants to recruit young ladies," laughed Karl

"That is a sexist remark..." Garcia began

"Albeit a true one." interposed Will

They all stiffened as there was a knock on the door. Garcia looked out through a spy-hole and quickly opened up. Neeta, now in her late teens or early twenties, walked confidently into the room.

"I am very sorry about this," said Garcia politely. Neeta didn't bat an eyelid as he frisked her expertly. He confiscated her mobile and switched it off. He didn't look that sorry.

"Quite understand." was Neeta's calm response.

Everyone was standing. They raised their fists. They said "Death to the Dictator!" I judged that they were not so loud the neighbours could hear. Neeta joined in as if she had expected this preamble.

Ygael, who seemed to be the leader, put an old-fashioned Video Cassette into an equally antiquated machine (if you don't know what I am talking about, ask your granny). The face of a woman in her middle years who would seem to have had a hard, austere life appeared on the screen.

"I am Sister Katherine." Xavier and Tilly exchanged glances. That name did seem to keep coming up in their adventures.

"I am a witness of the massacre of the hill tribes. I was

saved by gastroenteritis." She smiled at this irony. When she smiled her face was transformed. Underneath the austerity and the memory of suffering there seemed to be a kind of calm joy.

"I was confined to my bed and the nearest I got to the massacre was when Sister Margaret came to visit me. It seemed that for the first time in years, there was a plentiful supply of food in the village. The army had retreated from their base and left a large proportion of their supplies behind. The hill tribes had no reason to respect the army. The army had carte blanche to rape and murder and there were plenty of times when they had shot up villages apparently for the fun of it.

"I was in no position to keep any food down and soon Margaret was in a similar state. I assumed the gastroenteritis was particularly virulent in her case but soon she was in agony and vomiting blood. When I tried to help her or even to talk to her she flew into a rage. I have never seen her like it before. Within a short while she was dead. I had to bury her myself because the village, I thought, was deserted.

"People would often head for the hills in times of trouble when they thought the army was about to attack the village. I was wrong in thinking this was what had happened. As I became fit enough to explore I realised that people had not fled. They had died. From the look of them it seemed that they had perished in torment.

"When the soldiers did come, it was my turn to head for the hills. By then I was fit enough although I avoided eating anything that came from the army base. They came with flame-throwers and I watched them incinerating the bodies. They came with bulldozers and I watched them demolish the houses. They did not spare the Church. They dynamited it. I could do nothing but pray for their souls. I knew that I had to bear witness to what I had seen.

"If the state orders you to kill the poor you are under no obligation to obey that order. That is the message we have to get to the soldiers. The Dictator, sorry, the dictatorship must die."

Ygael turned the screen off and there was a silence in the room for a while.

Then it was Neeta who broke the silence.

"There is a difference in emphasis between 'Death to the Dictator' and 'Death to the Dictatorship.'"

Ygael dismissed this impatiently but Garcia thought it was worth impressing Neeta.

"Well killing the Dictator would be the same as the Narodny" ("Narodniks" Xavier couldn't resist saying) "killing the Tsar. They just ended up with another Tsar."

Ygael wasn't having any of it.

"If we kill the Dictator, the whole house of cards will collapse. So death to one means death to the other. And," he added slightly louder to put Garcia down, "surely the question now is what can we do with this. The tape is the only one in existence and the only eye-witness account we are likely to get.

Will was all for using social media. "If we can copy this and get it onto the internet then the message can be spread abroad. At least the emigre community will hear about it and news will filter back from them."

Neeta opposed this for her own reasons. "You would be signing Sister Katherine's death warrant by putting her face on the screen."

"It would be too late for that," Ygael interjected grimly.

Karl explained "She is already dead."

He turned to face Neeta "No the problem is that we haven't got the facilities to copy this for the internet." he continued.

Neeta was the youngest person present, "I do. VCR to CD. CD to MPEG4"

They looked at her as if she were speaking in Martian. She patiently explained what she meant. Then she impatiently repeated it.

Reluctantly they agreed. Seeing an opportunity, Garcia moved close to Neeta.

"I am very sorry about this but we cannot allow the video out of our sight. It is the only copy. I will accompany you however and make sure it is safe.

"We can also get to know each other better." he added more softly.

Neeta looked up at him as if getting to know Garcia better was the answer to a maiden's prayer.

The Mirror of Eternity followed them through the back streets as Neeta showed Garcia the way to her flat. He was teaching her a history she may already have known.

"The coup that brought the Dictator to power abolished all laws. I was in prison at the time and I was released into the army. Being drunk and disorderly doesn't usually carry the death penalty but I saw many of my fellow convicts die in battle against the various rebellions and attempted rebellions. We had a week's military training. We were up against rebels who had years of experience.

"What happened to the police? I never see any policemen." Neeta asked innocently.

"They all lost their jobs or at least their uniforms and a third of their pay. Most were re-employed directly by the Dictator in undercover roles. The policing was contracted to the former criminal gangs. The police infiltrated the gangs and kept them loyal to the Dictator."

Neeta modestly held back at the door and ushered Garcia in. Although they were in a poor part of town, the flat was luxurious with soft furnishings and deep pile carpets unobtainable to anyone on Garcia's income. Petra was already in the flat. She had clearly just emerged from the shower and she was wearing nothing but a towel. She gave Garcia a friendly kiss and accidentally dropped the towel. How they laughed!

Garcia has the night of his life

To give the devils their due, Garcia did have a night he remembered for the rest of his life. Neeta had a bottle of the local firewater which the twins drank as if they had been weaned on it. (*For all we know they had – narrator*).

Soon the three of them were naked on the bed and Neeta was licking his nipples while Petra was occupied further south. In time the firewater and the unaccustomed sexual athletics took their toll and Garcia was fast asleep. He hardly stirred when they handcuffed him to the metal bed-head The twins had coffee.

Petra drank half her cup then threw the rest into Garcia's face for a rude awakening. Garcia woke to see a beautiful girl with a beautiful smile and a lighted cigarette which she proceeded to use on his anatomy. Neeta sat on the bed with a notebook and took notes. They were indifferent to his suffering, they found it amusing if anything.

Consulting her notes, Neeta said "So you only have the names of the members of your own cell – Ygael, Karl and Will. You do not know where this.."she held up the video "came from but you believe it to be the only copy. Is that it?"

Petra slapped his face.

"Is that it?"

"Yes."

"Well we also have an interesting video. It was taken this evening."

Neeta used the remote and the wide-screen TV was full of a blow by blow replay of the twins and Garcia enjoying the earlier part of the evening.

"And that video is going to your wife and mother and to your brother and daughter for good measure. You really are a useless informant."

Petra put her hands around his throat and started expertly strangling him. She judged he was on the brink of unconsciousness when she appeared to have an idea.

"Unless you would like to find out more information for us? This offer expires in ten, nine, eight."

Garcia was gasping for breath but he managed to inhale "Yes." Then he said it normally a couple of times.

We watched as Garcia was taken in a car by two plain-clothed officers who dumped him in the scrub-land outside the town. He had to make his way home stark naked and have a go at explaining himself.

"I was robbed and beaten up" was the most likely explanation that occurred to him as he trudged through the dark night and he repeated it to himself like a mantra. He would have been a little surprised (although he had had enough surprises for one night) to see what the twins did next.

Neeta was as good as her word. She copied the video onto a CD and made further computer copies of it. She then posted these copies to anonymous email addresses.

In the end she held up the original and said to Petra, "Daddy will be very pleased with this." And there was still a laugh to be had between them when that name was used.

The Archbishop's Tomb

"So the prime projection," said Xavier, who talked like that at times, "is that one of the Dictator's mistresses had twin girls and he trained them as agents. One cell has now been infiltrated and it is possible the infection could spread, so to speak. Sister Katherine's account of the Massacre on video has not been destroyed. For their own reasons they have kept copies."

"What use is that to us?" Kaspar asked.

"Well we can access their copies through the use of passwords."

Xavier used the laptop to access one of the email accounts with a flourish and produced the relevant email.

"We can't use this. It would give away the fact we accessed their account." Kaspar objected.

"No it wouldn't. They don't know that Sister Katherine didn't send out more copies."

"You don't think they tortured her before they killed her?" Kaspar shook his head at Xavier's naivety

Xavier thought for a moment. "In that case she would have given away Ygael and the twin's operation would have been unnecessary. We know she died. The likelihood is that the

Dictator had her killed but she could have been caught in the crossfire rather than specifically captured and killed. I think we should ... oh bugger!

"Well that is all a bit academic. The file is encrypted,"

"The email system must have done it automatically. I didn't see her do anything to the file." Tilly said quickly. She was trying to make Xavier feel better. She did that a lot.

"Is there a credible émigré opposition?" she asked Kaspar, changing the subject.

He smiled wryly. "There are two. They are known as the Revolutionary Party and the Revolutionary Committee. That's the problem. They are at daggers drawn with each other. Arguably they spend more time fighting each other than opposing and exposing the Dictator. Those who say "Death to the Dictator" are barely on speaking terms with those who say "Death to the Dictatorship." Both factions are likely to end up vying for power if the Dictatorship is overturned and they have started that battle early.

"In fact, the only consistent opposition comes from people like Sister Katherine and priests who are close to the people. Some priests of course are close to the dictator or perhaps just scared. I don't know how you can use that information."

The look in Xavier's eye said that he knew how to use it. He suddenly declared we had done enough for one day and we should carry on tomorrow evening. Looking at his watch, Kaspar unnecessarily remarked "You mean this evening." It was 3.39 in the morning.

As soon as Kaspar had left we helped remove the chairs, revealing the pentacle.

"Goodbye darling, be careful." Tilly kissed kissed Xavier lightly, moved away and then came back for a good old-fashioned snog. I shook his hand.

(What follows is necessarily based on Xavier's evidence. The usual caveats apply)

Wolf-Dietrich had never been fond of St Sebastian's graveyard and the imposing mausoleum in which his mortal remains were buried. This was partly a natural desire not to think about his own demise but mainly because he thought it was thoroughly tasteless. To find himself dreaming that he was there was irritating to say the least.

"Xavier!" he called out loud. He knew that Xavier was more powerful than he was in this realm. Xavier had summoned him here once before[1] The rest of the discussion was very rapid because in the dreamscape the unlikely pair could read each other's minds. After Xavier had told Wolfie everything, Wolfie thought for a while. Then he began,

"Well I am not quite sure what a 'Dictator' is but I do hope you are not expecting me to get involved in this "democracy"

---

[1] I will just say "See Salt Wars". Most other references to the past could have the same footnote and you would soon tire of it.

nonsense of yours. I have told you often enough I consider it to be a fraud. The rich and powerful are still rich and powerful but the poor think they have a say in what goes on.

"But you will come to Mass at St Michael's?"

"Oh very well, Xavier. I have no objection to attending Mass with you but I fail to see how it will convince me."

The Massacre

The church of St Michael was in one of the poorest areas of town. In point of fact it was only half a mile from Ygael's house but Ygael was an unbeliever. Not so Garcia.

"He looks nervous." was all Wolfie had to say about him as they slid into the back row. They were dressed similarly to the rest of the congregation. Wolfie had refrained from objecting to twenty-first century clothing although he did not like it.

Xavier was seated so as to protect Wolfie from contact – or rather an embarrassing lack of contact – with anybody. Xavier's hard astral projection resembled a normal human being except for his exceptional strength. Wolfie was less substantial.

The first reading was from the book of Samuel from which you will realise this was in mid-January. (If you don't realise this, I am sure Wolfie would suggest you go to Mass more often) and the second was from Mark's gospel. Wolfie was surprised that the entire service was in the vernacular and he sat translating it into Latin silently. He was even more surprised by the homily.

"If I feed the poor, they call me a saint. If I ask why they are poor they call me a Communist." Father Simon suddenly had all of Wolfie's attention. So when Xavier pedantically explained what a Communist was, Wolfie glanced at him impatiently and he subsided.

"We are called upon to stand by the poor in solidarity. We see Christ in them. But we don't leave our brains aside. When we see suffering; when we see the gangsters ruling the streets. When we see the rich lording it over the poor. When we see the Dictator living in luxury while better people live in poverty.We have to ask why."

"He should be concerned about their souls not their bodies!" was Wolfie's furious thought.

As if he had caught it, Father Simon continued,

"I am concerned about the souls of the poor. I am also concerned about the souls of the soldiers. I am concerned about the souls of those children of the poor who put on a uniform and turn guns on their families and families like theirs. A man cannot serve two masters. A man cannot serve Satan and God. And a man cannot serve the country and the Dictator. An order to attack the poor is not a lawful order. Your conscience should tell you not to obey it. Our God is a God of justice and mercy. Anyone who believes in justice and mercy is already a servant of Jesus Christ whether they know it or not.
"

For the remainder of the Mass, Wolfie was seething with rage. To distract him, Xavier drew his attention to Garcia whose mind was a cauldron of conflicting emotions. It was impossible to read. Probably Garcia couldn't read it himself. When the time came to receive communion, Garcia hesitated and the people behind him waited politely until he eventually summoned up the courage to proceed. Wolfie couldn't participate and Xavier stayed with him. He had brought him here with a purpose.

After the final blessing, Father Simon was the first to die. He fell face down in the aisle and never moved again. Almost no one had time to cry out. Only those too young to have received communion were spared. They cried out and Xavier had his work cut out trying to get the children to safety. Garcia had made a swift exit but Xavier was too busy to pursue him. . Unable to assist, Wolfie stayed in his place and prayed fervently. The church was eerily silent.

As they left, Wolfie said bitterly, "Justice and mercy. I leave mercy to God. That man will receive justice with your help Xavier. And you will have my wholehearted support."

From the Diary of Wolf-Dietrich

I was settled down to bed with Salome. For once the children had been no bother and she was in an amorous frame of mind but enough about that.

No sooner was I asleep than I was summoned to the worst

possible place, the site of my wretched mausoleum

Torturer! Torturer indeed! By day, Xavier is the most efficient of torturers despite his aversion to actual torture. In my dreams, in the 'parallel universe' as he insists on calling it, he is torturing me! And I pay his wages. Well actually he doesn't get any but I am his employer after all.

I was outraged in St Michael's. What St Michael would make of it I hardly like to think. If that Father Peter were in Salzburg I would have a few words with him. "I excommunicate you" would be three of them. I suppose they would have to be in the vernacular because he showed no signs of even speaking Latin.

And then that disgraceful sacrilegious Massacre. I know autocracy is the way things are run in the world but this Dictator will have to go.

Splitters

Wolfie was wearing 21st century attire uncomfortably but he was determined to rise above it when we reconvened to use the Mirror of Eternity. Xavier diverted Kaspar when he tried to shake hands with Wolfie and quietly explained that, although potentially very useful, Wolfie was a little eccentric and it was inadvisable to touch him. Wolfie snorted wolfishly which seemed to confirm Xavier's point.

He sat next to Xavier and watched the screen fascinated. Xavier took us through the streets. The extreme poverty was evident. The plight of the children who had visible ribs and inadequate clothing against the night air was a familiar sight to Kaspar. The apartment we ended up in was as run-down as the rest on the outside. Inside it could not have been more different.However the luxury of the surroundings was eclipsed by what we saw.

Garcia was tied naked to the bed.

"Those angry red marks?" asked Tilly. They were all over his chest, concentrated around the nipples.

"Cigarette burns" said Xavier.

"And look at the semen stains," Kaspar remarked looking lower down. "They are conditioning him to like the pain."

Judging by the mess the twins had played the game of pleasure and pain for some time. There were sounds of heavy breathing and squeals as the two were enthusiastically acting out a steamy lesbian porno just out of Garcia's reach. Neeta seemed to be struggling just to keep a straight face but Petra seemed to be really into it.

"Are they trying to awaken Garcia's flagging libido?" asked Tilly innocently.

"They seem to be awakening it." Wolfie observed drily.

Neeta reached her hand out to caress Garcia, "Do you like it, Daddy?" And the pair dissolved in a fit of the giggles. Garcia looked as though he were wondering whether to join in the merriment but clearly decided not to.

They snuggled either side of Garcia. The way his arms were tied, it looked as if he were embracing them.

"We have something to show you, " whispered Petra in his ear. She flicked the remote and the TV came to life.

The view of St Michael's was from the ceiling and the camera dwelt on the death of Father Peter before panning out to show the horror of the Massacre in loving detail.

Xavier zoomed in to close-up on the remote. It was not a video they were watching. It was being broadcast live on TV.

"CCTV is everywhere," Kaspar explained. "Often people don't know where it is because the technology of concealment is state of the art, unlike health care or indeed anything else."

The commentator said that it was clearly the work of terrorists and the Dictator was ready to take difficult decisions about measures for public safety.

"Has anybody seen this man. There is a large reward for information leading to his capture."

Garcia gasped. Petra and Neeta grinned.

The camera showed grainy CCTV footage of what was clearly Garcia replacing the wine and wafers in the sacristy.

Petra leant over and whispered in his ear, "You are now a valuable man."

With a "don't get up" to the bound and gagged man, the girls got ready to go out for the night.

"The prime projection," Xavier began

"Why not just say 'I think it likely'" was Wolfie's rather peevish thought. Xavier gave a shamefaced grin and began again.

"I think it likely that Garcia has been deliberately fingered as a member of one faction and the intention is to inflame the tensions between them."

"Well yes," Kaspar was thoughtful, "People will think that the Dictator would never have put this on TV if it were his handiwork. And on the other hand, even those who think it really is his work, well they have had a warning, 'This will happen to you if you oppose me.'

"Father Peter was respected by both factions but the die-hards on either side would not baulk at killing him and seeking to put the blame on the Dictator. The Dictator has set his enemies against each other again.

Tilly remained unusually silent.

From the diary of Tilly

Xavier has gone off sex. Admittedly he paid close enough attention when Petra and Neeta were performing for Garcia so he has some interest still. I think he is so caught up in what is going on in the Dictatorship that he is half-hearted in his lovemaking at best. I will not stand for this. I want my oversexed Romeo back.

And now what really worries me is that he will want to send his hard astral projection to the Dictatorship. I am guessing that he will want to take Wolfie with him. The visit to the St Michael Massacre was intended to involve Wolfie and it seems to have worked. And the problem is that he won't want me. He will want the little lady to stay home out of some misguided sense of gallantry. Well I am not bloody well having that. If he goes, I go.

Ygael

(Note - The currency of the Dictatorship was officially called "Credits" but the people generally referred to it as "nards" meaning "bollocks" because of a well-remembered period of hyperinflation when the money was valueless.- Narrator)

"Listen. I can patch this rust-bucket up so it will keep going and it will only cost you 25 nards. It really needs 100 nards spending on it or it will be back for more work inside six months."

"Ygael. I have ten nards."

"Fifteen."

"No I mean I only have ten. I am not haggling, just telling you."

"Well there is nothing I can do for you so take your car away. You will have to push it though."

"What about ten nards now and the other five when I collect it tomorrow."

"The other five?"

"On my mother's life."

"Don't you ever let me hear you swear on your mother's life again. It is not yours to dispose of so keep it out of the negotiations."

"OK"

"And bring that five nards."

"You drive a hard bargain."

"I am robbing myself." The smile on Ygael's face belied the words but his retreating customer couldn't see it.

He bent over the engine and his expression altered again. This machine really was in an awful state.

"We are looking for a car." Ygael looked up to see the two strangers. One was a tall man in his early thirties, the other was a priest. Ygael had no great liking for priests.

"I do not sell cars." he said curtly and returned to his work. Xavier coughed to indicate they were still there. Ygael looked up.

"We thought you might know someone with a car to sell? Do you want to discuss it over a drink." Xavier looked pointedly at the bar across the street and added, "We'll pay."

Ygael had never had coffee with a priest before. He wouldn't pass up the opportunity to widen his experience.

"We are actually fasting at the moment." Xavier explained in response to Ygael's unasked question.

The bar was not crowded and Xavier had talked the barmaid into letting them occupy a table without the pair of them eating or drinking anything.

"Fasting! You know the poor have to fast most of the time." Ygael couldn't resist saying.

"I'm an atheist." He said apropos of nothing in particular.

"I don't believe in atheists." was Wolfie's response.

Xavier steered the discussion back to buying a car. He had drawn money from Kaspar's account. He had not quite got around to telling Kaspar about this arrangement as yet.

"We'll buy it. You service it. We pay you money. Does that sound a good idea to you?"

"Well Marcos comes in to this bar at lunchtime. If you are around I can introduce you to him. He's an atheist too." He looked aggressively at Wolfie who smiled back "But his car is kosher."

"Wasn't it terrible about that massacre at St Michael's." Xavier was fishing.

"Yes terrible. Terrorists so I heard on the wireless."

Xavier had the advantage of being able to read his mind. Ygael did not believe it was the work of terrorists but he was wary of saying anything incriminating in front of these two. Wolfie's priestly attire was a definite disadvantage in this negotiation but in a generally Catholic country they had decided it was advisable. Wolfie had been ordained a priest and therefore he was one now. He was certainly not an Archbishop in this reality.

A dark-haired man duly arrived in the bar and Ygael called him over.

"These two are looking for a car. This is Father Wolf and Xavier here is a lay brother of the order of St Katherine."

Surprisingly Marcos's tough features softened when Ygael said that.

"Ah yes. Like Sister Lam. " he said nodding.

However when it came to discussing price he was as tough as they come. "I bought this car for 250 nards but Ygael here has done a lot of work on it since then so I reckon at least 400."

Internally, however, he was reflecting that a car that cost him fifty nards was about to make him a fortune.

While they were haggling, a girl came into the bar. She was bone-thin and Xavier estimated that she was about twelve. Reading the surface of her mind he realised she was seventeen but made strenuous efforts to look younger. She was wearing a Nike t-shirt and very little else.

Marcos, whom she addressed as uncle, shooed her away. Wolfie called her over.

"What is your name, child?"

She looked at Marcos who nodded almost imperceptibly. She couldn't look Wolfie in the eye but developed an interest in the floor.

"Sarah, father."

As Wolfie framed another question she blurted out, "You know what I am father."

"Of course I do, you are a child of God."

Sarah suddenly smiled and looked up, "That is what Sister Lam said."

"We will have to meet this Sister Lam"

Another barely perceptible head gesture from Marcos sent Sarah off to solicit the attention of other drinkers at the bar.

They went out into the street to look at the car which turned out to be a Peugeot 106. Xavier tried it out and it seemed to be in good running order. What it wasn't was kosher. Marcos himself did not know the provenance of the vehicle but in a country without licensing authorities or MOTs many of the cars were of dubious origin. There were no police to arrest them and the gangs were only interested in car theft from a strictly professional point of view.

Xavier realised immediately that Marcos was a minor member of a gang but his job was running girls like Sarah. He was selling the car on his own behalf. He filed this piece of information away for future use.

Ygael suggested that they try "certain streets" if they wanted to find Sister Lam.

"They are not very nice streets, Father. It is not good for your reputation to be seen there."

"But it is good for Sister Lam?"

"Well I will say no more. I will give this car a thorough check for you. You did pay rather a lot for it."

He secretly thought they were idiots to let Marcos rook them but he adjusted his prices for servicing accordingly.

Hanging around the garage and trying to engage Ygael in conversation turned out to be a hiding to nothing. Following his directions, Xavier dropped Wolfie at St Michael's before setting off for the red-light district.

Xavier was just another foreign tourist kerb-crawling and he politely declined a number of invitations from girls similar in age to Sarah. Each was under the watchful eye of their own "uncle".

As night was falling he witnessed an incident.

A big car drew up outside a house and a very young girl was forcibly ejected. The car then sped away. There was a sound of laughter from the college boys inside. They had not paid.

The uncle was furious.

"I ought to break your bloody arm you stupid little bitch."

He grabbed her arm and raised his fist.

A figure dressed in brown sensible clothes intervened

grabbing his arm. The man seemed to be astonished that the woman had such strength.

She wasn't berating him. She was talking calmly, Xavier could not hear the words but the man eventually calmed down and let go of the girl. The woman then talked to the girl and hugged her. Then astonishingly she hugged the uncle too. It was not clear what he thought about this but she left him no choice.

The woman turned away and Xavier caught sight of her face in the light of a street lamp.

"Tilly?

Sister Lam

(This is from Tilly's evidence so it can be taken as accurate)

Tilly arrived at the Hollands' family residence. It was a ramshackle end of terrace house that had seen better days. She found the door locked and there was no answer to the bell so she went round the back. The back door was never locked, in fact the lock didn't work. Terrence had promised to fix it in 1988 and would get round to it "in due course".

She went through the echoing house, which appeared to be empty. The room she sought was unlocked with the disregard for security she had come to accept as the norm. Pushing open the door she noticed that someone had altered the pentagram. The arcane symbols had been replaced with the three words "Amor Vincit Omnia" in Geert Hollands' flowing script.

That was not the first thing she noticed of course. The first thing she noticed was the naked body of Geert Hollands spread-eagled elegantly inside the pentacle. She was just thinking that Geert scrubbed up quite well for a woman of her age and then going on to wonder exactly what her age was when Geert awoke.

She was one of those people, like her adopted son Xavier, who woke to full consciousness like a wild animal. She was ready for fight or flight in a split second. In this case she was able to politely offer Tilly a cup of coffee.

"Or tea if you insist." as she put it.

"What were you, er."

"Doing?" Geert offered archly. "Well that's for me to know and for you to keep your nose out of, Tilly. Let's just say that hard astral projections are just as much fun for people who are grown up as they are for young whipper-snappers like you and Xavier.

"I take it that you have come here to see Terrance. He will not be back until later. Until then we can play backgammon." It was not a question.

Geert showed no sign of putting any clothes on so Tilly just shrugged and tried to remember how to win at Backgammon.

By the time Geert was ten pounds up, Tilly was pleased to hear Terrance blundering into the house.

He looked at Geert and gave an "I know what you've been up to" smile and turned to Tilly.

"Well, it is always nice to see you but am I right in thinking a) Xavier is in trouble and b) that he is in his sealed room and c) you are going to try to help him?"

Geert muttered "Sherlock Holmes."

Tilly just said "Yes, yes and yes. I don't want to inconvenience you but it will require the use of..." and she gestured towards the room where Terrance's Mirror of Eternity and the pentacle were.

Terrance looked at his wife, "Geert?"

"Well I couldn't care less." She looked daggers at Tilly and picked up the backgammon board. "Thank you for the game" was her parting shot before leaving the two of them together.

Terrance helped set the scene with incense and candles. He lingered to see if Tilly was going to disrobe but after a slight hesitation he left. Tilly locked the door and left the key in it. This was not much in the way of security but it was better than nothing.

Later Terrance was sitting in his study when he noticed that he couldn't quite see one of his book cases. There was a sort of mist in front of it. As he was looking directly at it, the mist resolved itself into the form of Tilly. She was naked which he found gratifying but she had some experience of astral projection and she rapidly clothed herself in sensible clothes and flat shoes appropriate for the role she had chosen. She then made an unusual request.

Nobody, least of all Terrance, knew why he possessed a

gun. If the police had known how useless his security was they would doubtless have confiscated it. However his incompetence extended to not registering it as well so they had no knowledge of it. Tilly thought for a moment and then asked him to shoot her. He consented to shoot her in the hand "just in case."

"Come on, Terrance. I could take a hundred bullets in the dreamscape without ill effect."

"Are you sure?"

"Well this experiment will verify that, but I am pretty sure. I have put my hand, well this hand, not my hand I suppose, in a candle flame before."

Closing his eyes and squeezing the trigger, Terrance winced at the noise. Then he took the opportunity to hold Tilly's hand and examine it.

"You are going somewhere pretty damned dangerous aren't you?"

"Well hopefully not for me. And I am sure I will be able to help Xavier." Her parting shot made the old atheist smile.

"Pray for us."

And with those rather appropriate words, Sister Lam was born.

The Red Light District

In a dark back alley-way in Capital City in the Dictatorship a mist formed and rapidly assumed the shape of Sister Lam in her drab brown clothes with her sensible brown shoes. Her mind chose this moment to recall how Kaspar had described Capital City. "They would cut your throat for the clothes you stand up in." Tilly had dismissed this, saying, "Well the clothes would be covered in blood wouldn't they?" At the time she had no thought that she would be going there herself.

She arrived in January of the year in which Wolfie and Xavier were coming. This gave her six months. Time goes differently in the dreamscape and she expected that period to pass overnight so she wouldn't inconvenience Geert for long. She smiled as she speculated about what Geert was getting up to but her mind was brought sharply back to the here and now by a very sharp knife. One hand held her shoulder and the other held the knife to her throat.

"Give me your money."

Lucas had a very direct way of approaching tourists.

"I don't have any money."

"Don't lie to me. A tourist with no money. Don't be silly."

"I don't have any money. I think your wife, sorry your girlfriend, Connie would be annoyed if you killed me. I have no money and you won't get fifty cents for my clothes. I am a sister of the order of St Katherine. We do not carry money."

Lucas was groping her breasts, seeking some compensation for the meeting. This stopped when she said, "Your mother's name was Katherine. She wouldn't want you doing this. She brought you up to have respect."

She took hold of Lucas's wrist and gently but firmly pushed him away. The knife dropped from numb fingers. Lucas's bravado melted into the darkness. He was clearly terrified at **what** he had found here.

"You are in league with the devil!"

"If anyone I am in league with St Katherine, Lucas." The use of his name was the last straw. He tried to cross himself but his wrists were in a vice-like grip. Tears started in his eyes.

"Let me go."

"Not yet, Lucas. You need me." He was trembling now.

"Are you a ghost?"

"Did I feel like a ghost? Now be calm, Lucas. I mean you no harm. In your heart you know this."

She watched the thought taking a hold of his frazzled brain. At exactly the right moment she gave him a hug.

"Now you are going to help me, Lucas."

He was dumbstruck, a state he had never experienced before.

She had to repeat herself, "Now you are going to help me, Lucas. Show me the way to the red light district."

She saw that he needed an explanation. "The place where the prostitutes and their uncles wait for tourists in cars."

"You don't want to go there. It is not the place for you, Sister." He said eventually.

"Nevertheless that is where I am going."

Lucas took her through the streets until they were close but he was not going to that area himself. What if he were seen? What would Connie do to him?

Sister Lam saw all this in his thoughts. He received the most unusual request a mugger can receive.

"Give me money."

Without a thought he handed over a fistful of nards. He turned on his heel and left Sister Lam to make her own way.

It had rained here and the street lamps were reflected in the puddles. It was one of the better-lit streets but the lamps were all on one side, leaving the other pavement in the darkness. Sister Lam knew perfectly well that she would be bound to this reality if she ate or drank anything or had sex. Looking around, she reflected that it was not a reality she would like to be bound to. Nevertheless she made her way to a café on the shady side of the street.

To begin with she was alone and sat over a coffee she would have to dispose of somehow. Then two girls came in.

One was wearing a T shirt and nothing else. The other had a remarkably short skirt and fishnet tights. She was topless. They looked very young. They both eyed Sister Lam with suspicion. This became more acute when she offered to buy them a meal.

"What do you want?" asked Shelly (she also went by the names Sheila and Suki)

Their suspicion peaked when Sister Lam answered them in a foreign accent.. "I am just tired. I thought you looked hungry.

Sorry if I'm wrong."

They were not too suspicious to refuse free food. They took the food and then talked to each other as if Sister Lam were not there.

"It's OK for you. Nobody messes with 'The Man'" Shelly said.

They both laughed at this. Lucy (aka Delia) had an uncle called 'The Man'

"He thinks he's the capo dei capi" said Lucy

"or at least the 'uncle of all the uncles'" teased Shelly

"He gave me this." Lucy spoke as if revealing a gift. She showed Shelly a fresh bruise on her thigh. Then she looked up to see Sister Lam looking at her.

"What are you looking at?"

By way of answer she got the café owner to soak a cloth in water and gave it over without a word. Lucy applied it to the bruise.

"My uncle never gave me one like that" Shelly continued.

"Mitch is soft. Everybody says so. If they don't bruise you they can't be strong enough to look after you."

"Say that a bit louder," Shelly said, looking out of the window. Lucy fell silent

Mitch opened the door a crack. The one word "business" was enough to get Shelly outside. He scowled at Sister Lam and she smiled gently in response. He had no idea what to do with that response so he gave Shelly an unnecessary shove out into the street.

When Lucy was alone she was slightly more forthcoming but Sister Lam was very careful not to overstay her welcome.

She walked down to the far end of the street and back again. There was one other girl on this stretch apart from Lucy and Shelly. Her name was Jenny (or occasionally Maria). She was wearing black tights and a blouse open to the waist. Her uncle had no name but he was known as Doctor. Once in a while a car would stop for him rather than for her and a brief transaction involving his prescribing skills would take place.

Cars, expensive cars, cruised around the area. The drivers would often ask the age of the girl and the girls would aim for an age as low as possible with credibility. In general the uncles were just a dark presence in the background. The girls got into the cars after haggling about money. A girl was worth about fifteen nards. This was pocket money for the tourists. It would have been a lot of cash for the girls to hold but it didn't stay out of uncle's hands for long.

Sister Lam was unfailingly polite to them, even when, especially when, they were disparaging about her. She would give them time to get used to her presence.

She had a stroke of luck when she got back to the café The man behind the counter had changed. It was an older man, Charles, who turned out to be the owner. Charles lived above the shop and he had a spare room for "someone such as yourself."

It required no mind-reading skills to work out what old Charles wanted. For some reason he was not put off by the fact she was a lay sister. Possibly he just misunderstood the word 'lay' but the room would be invaluable for her.

"And it is twenty five nards a week."

Lucy made a snorting noise.

"You old crook. It is worth ten if it is worth anything."

"I've got twelve" Sister Lam said. "And I can wash up." which turned out to be a deal-maker as far as Charles was concerned. He made some half-hearted attempts to extract sexual favours from Sister Lam but in truth he was relieved to fail because he doubted his prowess.

She bought Lucy, who had an amazing appetite despite her emaciated appearance, another plate of sandwiches. The bread was thin and white and Charles spread it very thinly with a pale paste from a huge plastic container. To this he added the meat of who knew what animal of who knew what antiquity. It did not look healthy but Lucy wolfed it down anyway.

In her tiny room, Sister Lam wrote her diary. She had no need of sleep in the dreamscape. Some of her thoughts were less holy than you might have expected.

From the Diary of Sister Lam

I want to kill Garcia. If I could do that now, I would save the lives of all those people in Saint Michael's. I know Doctor Katherine would tell me that is not the way and in any case

Garcia is a victim. I am just setting down the thought rather than pretending I don't feel it. I know my lover, Xavier, (how I enjoy setting those words on the page!) would tell me about temporal paradoxes until the cows go out and come home at the same time. And dear Terrance would do the same to the accompaniment of his foul pipe. What does he put in it? Superannuated socks I think.

Thinking of them just reminds me of how far from home I am here. The room has a view over the street. There are more girls now but the uncles keep their territory strictly marked out. The girls use the harsh glare of the street lamps to show their bodies to the tourists. They have practised poses. Jenny for example walks around quite normally in high heels when there were no cars in the street. When there are customers in the offing she walks awkwardly like a little girl in mummy's high heels. It seems to work.

More of the tourists seem to be drunk judging from the noise. Still what do they care? Drunk driving and child abuse are crimes back home, not here. How is it that they cannot see what they are doing. "would some power the giftie gie us to see ourselves as others see us." My sins must be as clear as day to other people. I'm the one who can't see them.

Come to think, the local firewater would probably numb their consciences in the same way as it seems to numb everything else. It is a wonder they can still perform.

I need have no doubts of the fact they can. Some don't

bother to drive away. They just park and take the girl in the back.

Appointment with the Doctor

The café opened early. Sister Lam met the Doctor and Jenny who were the last to finish their night shift. Jenny was complaining about her last customer.

"His breath smelt like something died in there."

"Halitosis." He brought out the word with a flourish, as if he expected applause, "It is usually just bacteria from not brushing their teeth. Eat a mint or something."

"What use is that. It is his breath that smells not mine."

"Yes but you will taste it less with a mint."

"See how I look after her. " This last was addressed at Sister Lam, when there was no response, he went on, "Look Sister, this is a useless street-walker. In a couple of years she will be too old. I look after her. I protect her and I would never harm her."

Jenny looked down and he amended his story, "I only hit her if she really needs it, if she has been disobedient or something like that. And I don't leave marks, I'm very careful about that.

Sister Lam was surprised to see that in Doctor's mind, he believed everything he was saying. Even more surprisingly, he regarded himself as a doctor.

"You're a Doctor, Phil?"

He didn't notice her use of his real name. In his defence he was tired after a long night on the street.

"Well here I am. Back in my own country I was struck off because some stupid little girls complained about the way I handled them. Here in the dictatorship there is none of that nonsense. Anybody can be a doctor and anybody is. Here I can prescribe heroin or cocaine for anyone who needs it.

"And I doctor to you don't I?" He put his hand around Jenny's throat and slapped her face three times. Jenny didn't bat an eyelid. There was an ugly red mark on her cheek which slowly faded. There was a look in Doctor Phil's eye which Sister Lam didn't like. To read his mind she needed to love him and he wasn't making that any easier. What she could see of his mind showed a catalogue of child abuse. He couldn't see anything wrong with it.

Something had made him this way.

"I was brought up in Sussex." She said by way of changing the subject.

Doctor Phil sneered. "Brought up? Brought up" he mimicked, "Well people like me are not 'brought up'. You either survive or you don't. My mother was a drug addict and my father – well who the devil was he?"

"I could have got this one," he indicated Jenny, "hooked on H. A lot of the girls here are on the needle. It would have shortened her useful life so I didn't do it. I have to take tough decisions."

"You were in care?"

For a minute it looked as if Doctor Phil wasn't going to answer. His face darkened and he just looked dog-tired. Eventually he said, as if to himself, "Stupid thing to call it. They only put you in care if they don't care. Nobody cared about us. We didn't care about them. Right, Jenny?"

When Jenny remained silent he slapped her face again.

"Right." was all he got from her. She was eager to get to sleep.

"OK Sister Lam, Charles has been telling everybody about you. So will we be seeing you again? Will you be around here, doing good?" He said the last two words like swear words.

Sister Lam just looked at him. Somehow that seemed to calm him down. Then she said quietly, "It must have taken a lot of will-power to work your way through college and qualify as a doctor. I find it admirable.

"Pity you couldn't keep your hands off little girls." She didn't say that last sentence out loud.

Jenny's Story

Later that day, Jenny was sitting alone in the café over the inevitable coffee She always described it as sweet as sin, strong as Hercules and as black as Hell. Sister Lam came in from the kitchen drying her hands. Charles didn't run to luxuries like rubber gloves and she was glad her real life hands wouldn't be affected.

"Oh it's you." Jenny remarked without enthusiasm.

After a while she added, "the smell of washing-up liquid

always reminds me of my mum. She disappeared after the Miranda contest and in the first place I came to Capital City to find her.

"Miranda contest?"

"For Christ's sake, Sister, sorry but well for somebody's sake, don't you know anything? The soldiers came to the village. They didn't come to shoot the men, rape the women or levy taxes. They put up posters with pictures of Miranda. You know Miranda?"

Sister Lam nodded. She could see the image of Miranda in Jenny's mind.

"And they organised a Miranda look-alike contest. Nobody trusted them but the prizes were tempting. Well people always said my mum looked like the Dictator's mistress, Miranda. She was the same height but to be perfectly honest the rest was done with make-up and hair dye but it was a fairly small village. To cut the long story short, she won. It turned out her prize was a trip to Capital City.

"She had to go alone. When dad protested the soldiers hit him around the head with a rifle butt. That was true to form at least.

"She never came back. I got it into my head that whatever I did I was going to go to Capital City and find her. There was a train to Capital City every week from the village and I just got on it.

"I didn't steal the money for the train fare but then I didn't exactly pay for the trip either. I just hid in the toilet every time a ticket inspector came along. Then I met a lovely man on the train who insisted on paying my fare so I didn't get into trouble. He bought me a meal and gave me drinks. Well I had never had alcohol before because my parents thought I was too young. Anyway he said it was all right. I didn't like the firewater all that much to be honest with you but I downed it quickly like he said.

"When I arrived at the station I felt a bit woozy and he took me to a flat to lie down for a minute. I must have passed out though. When I woke up somebody had walked off with all my clothes and tied me to the bed for good measure.

"That was when I met the doctor. He came in and looked me over. He paid the man from the train some money and he rescued me. Of course he then said that I had to work off the money and that's what I am doing here. Fair's fair. I keep working but the interest on the money keeps going up. I don't understand it myself but it seems I owe the doctor more each month.

"Listen, Sister Lam, I have been working every day since I came here and I haven't had a chance to look around at all. I don't have a picture of my mum but like I said she looks a bit like Miranda so that will have to do. If you find her I will be eternally grateful."

The look of hope in her eyes made Sister Lam agree to this apparently hopeless task.

The Man

"You are going to listen to me, you bitch." The Man punctuated the remark with a slap around Sister Lam's face. It didn't hurt, or course, she chose not to be hurt by it.

She slowly and deliberately presented the other cheek and he slapped that too.

Lucy had been brought along to witness the lesson. She couldn't help herself, she laughed. The laugh was quickly suppressed but it was enough to enrage The Man. He went to backhand Lucy and found he couldn't move his arm. Sister Lam was holding it, saying "I think that is enough."

The thought of arm-wrestling a nun was just too absurd for The Man to contemplate. He also had a suspicion that he would not win. He shouted abuse for a while which Sister Lam took calmly.

(*I have deleted most of the expletives, they get repetitive - narrator*) "You will leave these useless girls alone. They are none of your business. You will not encourage Jenny's ridiculous idea of finding her mother. We are nothing to do with you. Leave us alone."

"You're an admirer of Miranda aren't you?"

"I am a patriot."

"So you are an admirer of the Dictator?"

"You know nothing. The Dictator just **is** without the likes and dislikes of me. The beautiful Miranda stays the hand of the Dictator. She protects the people. Everybody knows that."

Sister Lam could see that The Man actually half-believed this. Yet he told himself that he believed in nothing. She took a decision on the spot.

"You want me to leave. I will go but I will return because there are people here who need me."

The Man spat. "People. What people?"

"You for a start."

He sneered but he was sneering at her back.

Charles hastened outside and spoke to her quietly. He didn't want to disagree with The Man in public.

"Come back soon. Those girls like having you around. Nobody else cares for them. And I need your dish-washing skills." He added with a sly smile.

Sister Lam nodded. It was as good as a promise.

Saint Miranda's

Wandering through the streets of Capital City, Sister Lam found herself outside a baroque church. She noticed that it was called the Church of Saint Miranda and the priest was a Father Alon. She made up her mind to go in and pray. There was a statue of Saint Miranda and a plethora of candles glittered in the gloom. It was the brightest part of the old church. She joined the throng of worshippers who were praying before the statue.

She found it easy to eavesdrop on their thoughts.

"Please help me find my brother. He disappeared six months ago and we don't know how to manage without his income."

"Please keep the Dictator from taking my shop away from me."

"Please keep the Dictator from..." seemed to be the prefix of most of their requests. Some firmly believed Saint Miranda could help them. Some were sceptical but thought anything was worth a try.

She noticed the priest. He was in his early forties and he looked as though he had not been bowed down by life in The Dictatorship. He did not seem to have that hopeless look in his eye which Sister Lam had seen so many times in the streets. He was sitting quietly on the edge of the crowd and she made up her mind to talk to him when the opportunity arose. By one of those senses which are not usually listed he realised that she was looking at him and turned around and smiled.

"You look as if you could use a coffee."

"Thank you but I am fasting. I would like to talk though."

When they were in the sacristy, she began,

"There isn't a Saint Miranda is there?"

"Well outside The Dictatorship there isn't but there are five St Miranda's churches in Capital City alone. I didn't name the church, I've only been here two years. You have seen the way the people look to St Miranda to stay the hand of" he couldn't resist looking behind him when he said it, "the tyrant?"

"Mmm but does she do it?"

"The people believe she does. I am not sure. I know that

somebody has to stay his hand though."

"You must trust me a lot to say that out loud."

"Well I have heard of your work with the street girls, Sister Lam. You have made a good beginning there."

Father Alon seemed to take an unholy delight in Sister Lam's look of surprise.

"Not much takes you unawares does it? Perhaps a surprise does you good.

"You see although I cannot read minds I hear a lot of, well, let's call it gossip. And you, I am told, have the strength of a bull, a particularly strong bull at that and they say you have powers of mind which would get you burnt as a witch in less enlightened times. People were bound to talk about you.

"Oh and your washing-up is highly regarded." he added

"By whom?"

"By my cousin Charles for one. Charles likes to talk rather more than to think of course but his heart is more-or-less in the right place."

"Charles is your..."

"cousin. Yes. But sister you are not using your powers of mind or you would already know that."

"I can't..."

"read my mind?" Father Alon's expression was one of amused innocence.

She sat back and smiled. "Yes. You are reciting the breviary internally while you are talking to me. I had a friend."

She paused. Was Wolfie actually a friend? Sort of, she concluded. "who could do that sort of thing.

"But don't you trust me, Father"

"I am planning to trust you with a secret which could cost me my life, Sister. I just want a little privacy. Priests don't always manage to be thinking priestly thoughts, you know."

She nodded. She was beginning to believe this brave priest had important information for her and that her coming to this particular church was more than mere chance.

"There are a group of women who meet here. Some people call them the sisters of Saint Miranda, others are less polite about them. They meet at this church when nobody else is around, including me. Well officially I am on the premises but I leave them to their devices. I know that they gather here and I know that their prayers are not made silently.

"Do you know what a mantilla is?"

Flustered by the question, Sister Lam was unnecessarily emphatic in her confirmation. She thought he would explain it anyway. Instead he waited.

"It's the significant figures in a number." she said eventually.

"That is a mantissa. And you are teasing me, Sister. Should you be doing that?"

"Anyway I have seen a woman wearing a mantilla veil who also attends these meetings at times. She listens intently to what this group are saying but she talks to nobody and she keeps herself muffled up whatever the weather. It seems to be important to her that nobody sees her."

"And I think we can both make an educated guess as to who she is. Or perhaps who she would have them think she is." Sister Lam concluded and Father Alon smiled agreement.

Extract from the Diary of Father Alon of St Miranda's church

A good day for the Dictatorship, well for the country at least. And possibly a very bad day for the Dictator. The man known as Kaspar said that Tilly Hollands would arrive but he didn't say when and this speed is astonishing. I can only assume that Xavier and Wolfie must be working undercover somewhere. She certainly didn't mention anything about them and that was probably a reasonable precaution.

My experience of the resistance is that they are pretty futile. If I have a couple of hours to spare I can discuss whether "Death to the Dictator!" was preferable to "Death to the Dictatorship!" but there are a lot of parishioners and a lot of needs to attend to so on the whole I don't.

I have high hopes of Sister Lam, as she is known now. I wonder if the Wolf and the Lamb get on. Well we shall see. Tomorrow is the usual day for the Sisters of Saint Miranda and Sister Lam will be there. She seems audacious and self-confident. She confessed to me this evening and of course I cannot divulge her confession but I can set down here that some of it was incomprehensible.

The Sisters of Saint Miranda

The women gathered in the church. They seemed to be from a range of backgrounds. Some of them were obviously rich, judging by their clothes they were wearing but there was no sign of jewellery of any kind. This was probably a wise precaution because the streets were not safe.

They all welcomed Sister Lam with open arms and smiles. When the church was about half full, they began with general prayers which she joined in. Then one woman, one of the poorer ones judging by her clothes and rough hands, stood up and she turned to the statue of Saint Miranda. The rest of them turned the same way.

"Saint Miranda, sister of our sorrows and guardian of our fate. I bring you my humble petition. I fear for my daughter who is in danger from a grave illness. I pray that you will guard and protect her as you have guarded and protected us all."

"Saint Miranda, we beg you to hear our prayer." The other women responded.

She was no sooner seated than another woman rose, "Saint Miranda, sister of our sorrows and guardian of our fate. My husband is in despair since he lost his job at the factory. I beg you to help him to find hope and to find work."

"Saint Miranda, we beg you to hear our prayer." The other women responded. And so the supplications went on. Many of them wanted to find missing relatives, usually men and some children, who had disappeared with the assistance of the Dictatorship. Others wanted to protect their lives and property from the gangsters who ruled the streets. One rather strange intervention was from a woman who thanked the Saint for the sugar. The other women looked at her with disapproval and there were no further thanks offered. Sister Lam wondered what this might signify.

She had noticed the woman in the black mantilla and she tried to get closer to her without being too obvious. The other women carefully acted as if she wasn't there although they were unfailingly friendly to everyone else. They made sure that she heard all their requests though. She seemed to be paying close attention although she contrived with some skill to keep her face always in shadow.

Sister Lam resolved to follow her after the service ended. She almost missed her because she slipped out rather sharply. She didn't adjust her clothing on leaving the church but hastened through the streets avoiding any other pedestrians.

Sister Lam was just turning a street corner when she saw the woman in the black mantilla slip into a doorway. For want of any other plan, Sister Lam followed. The door opened and she was temporarily blinded by the bright light inside. Strong hands dragged her inside. The woman was there, divesting herself of the mantilla and her companion was instantly recognisable as Neeta.

Extract from Petra's Diary

I always enjoy going to listen to the Miranda Whores having a whine in the church. Today there was an added bonus when that stupid bitch Lam followed me home like a Lam to the slaughter. It was the work of a minute to drag her inside. Neeta and I took it in turns to beat her but frankly she is the most disappointing prisoner I have ever had.

For a start, she seems to be impervious to pain. There is something weird about the way the stupid cow just takes whatever we can think up and she makes no attempt to escape. I have a lot of ways of discouraging escapees but I haven't needed any of them. Then when we went out for the evening, leaving her tied to the bed, we came back to find her fully clothed and sitting at the table reading the paper. If it had been me I would have legged it.

I don't know what to do with her but Neeta has a few suggestions which we might try. For instance if we torture Garcia in front of her and appeal to her compassion. Well it is worth a try and it will be fun anyway. If only she knew, Garcia is such a pain-slut now that he would not like it if she started naming names to stop his torture.

And we have got no information out of her. Not a sausage. Well that's no use. I will probably have to make something up for the report now. And Daddy wouldn't like that, if he knew about it. Neeta is such a big fat grass that she will tell him if she can. If she can without implicating herself that is.

Raindrops

"Well this one has fallen a lot further than the others and picked up a lot of carbon dioxide in the process, making itself into a weak acid. That one is running down that guy's nose so it looks as though he has a bad cold and that one..."

Sister Lam took a pause to remind herself why she was imagining rainfall. She was impassively watching as the twins alternately rewarded and punished Garcia. What had started out as a way to break Sister Lam had turned into an entertainment in its own right when it became apparent it was having no effect on her.

On the one hand she still wanted to kill Garcia no matter how many temporal paradoxes this would cause. She was keen to keep this information from the twins. On the other hand Garcia was undoubtedly enjoying himself.

So she visualised a raindrop running down a window pane and watched as it merged with another.

Then her concentration was broken.

A tall dark-haired woman in her mid forties wearing the uniform of a captain in the Dictator's army walked into the scene of lust and depravity as if it was more-or-less what she expected.

"Don't you bloody knock?" was the enquiry of Petra as she hastily adjusted her clothing.

"Knock? I'll knock your bloody teeth out if you don't watch

yourself."

Petra smiled sweetly and meekly offered the captain a chair.

"Get this stupid bitch out of here." She gestured and Neeta removed Sister Lam from the room. She put a pair of heavy handcuffs on her wrists and forced her into a pair of headphones playing rubbish at an ear-splitting volume – one of their favoured torture techniques in fact.

There is very little point in removing someone from the room so they cannot hear you if they have the power to read your mind. Nevertheless the music was a distraction. Sister Lam concentrated on the handcuffs. She knew from her training from Doctor Katherine that she could break them. Whatever strength she needed she would find.

She thought back to the candle Doctor Katherine had used. She visualised her hand in the flame. The pain in her mind. And how she had learned to switch if off. She took a deep breath, quite unnecessarily she mocked herself. The handcuffs broke apart. They had a good go at breaking her wrists in the process but she was free.

The headphones came off.

"I've got a job for this"

"Garcia." Neeta volunteered.

"I don't care what his bloody name is. His name will be shit after he does what I want him to do."

Captain Brand outlined Garcia's role in the plot to wipe out

Father Simon with maximum collateral damage. She actually laughed at the phrase.

"Father Simon..." Garcia began.

"Oh it talks does it? Now shut the fuck up and I don't want another word out of you. And you two are supposed to have trained this piece of shit. Fucking useless, the pair of you."

Nobody else spoke to the twins like that.

"Captain Brand. I assure you that he will do as he is told."

"Well he'd better. Now let's go over the plan again shall we..."

Captain Brand went over the plan. She made sure the twins understood it all. She had no interest in Garcia. It was their job to get him to do it. All the time behind the words she was thinking, "I hate having to use this Satanic pair. I told the Dictator that they should have been strangled at birth and as a reward he made me their handler. As if anyone would want to handle them! Well, come to think of it, Garcia would obviously like the idea but then he's rebel scum and they screw anything. This whole place revolts me."

And out loud, "Now this prisoner of yours. Have you got a single useful bit of information from her?"

It was Petra who answered. She had an unaccustomed tone of respect. "She is called Sister Lam and she attended the Sisters of Miranda meeting at the Church. We have had our eyes on Father Alon for some time but he seems to be clean. He allows the sisters to use the church but then he makes himself scarce when..."

"Yes I know all that. I read your reports, crap though they generally are. What new information do you have?"

There was a pause and then "Fuck all. As I thought." It seemed odd to hear such language in such a high-class tone. Letting her contempt for the twins colour her language, perhaps.

"Well I will have to deal with her myself."

Sister Lam was excited by these words. She wanted to get higher up the food chain than the twins. "And I won't be tempted to kill Garcia." she said out loud.

The door banged open and Captain Brand took in the broken handcuffs and the removed headphones.

"Eavesdroppers never hear anything good about themselves, my dear." She said with mock kindness she put her arm around Sister Lam's shoulders and propelled her towards the waiting car. In the back of the chauffeured limo she held Sister Lam's face in her surprisingly soft but strong hands. "You will tell me everything you know dear. Believe me in the end you will want to make things up so you have more to tell me." She expertly blindfolded Sister Lam and casually felt and pinched and punched her body, seeking for what she thought of as "buttons." She liked to know her prisoners' buttons.

She was confounded by a prisoner who seemed to have none but as the journey progressed and the physical probing became more aggressive, Sister Lam sensed that Captain Brand was intrigued by the challenge. It was a characteristic of close servants of the dictator that they tried to shed names. Captain Brand never once let on what her Christian name was for example. In her own mind her first name was "Captain".

In her mind, Sister Lam called her "Jo" but that was the most private of jokes. Antagonising a torturer is not generally regarded as good policy. Sister Lam was confident that she could take any amount of pain. To be precise she wouldn't feel it in this body. She also knew from Xavier that the most effective torturers target the mind not the body.

She was hustled out of the car and when the blindfold was removed she was in a bare stone room with a desk and one chair. She was stripped naked and she imagined it was cold although she couldn't feel it. Captain Brand liked to think of herself as a tireless interrogator. She sat comfortably in the chair and began the questions.

"Now dear, tell me all about yourself."

"My name is Sister Lam."

When it became apparent that was all she was going to say, Captain Brand continued.

"In the end you will tell me everything. Nobody **wants** you to suffer. You might as well tell me everything now."

"My name is Sister Lam."

She paused long enough for Captain Brand to think that was all before adding, "I don't have a rank or serial number."

Time passed. Questions about the Sisters of Miranda and Father Alon were interspersed with increasingly vicious attempts to find her "buttons" After three hours the tireless Brand was beginning to tire of this.

"Well time for phase one. I am off to have a nice meal. You are not. Quin!"

The final shout brought a man Sister Lam tried very hard not to think of as the ugliest individual she had ever clapped eyes on. His age was hard to determine but he was old. All of his features seemed to be arranged in the wrong configuration and it was apparent that he had an aversion to soap and water.

She was given a room with a view. It was a dark and damp cell and all the light came from a tiny semi-circular barred window which looked out onto a square in The Dictator's compound. The entertainment consisted of watching the feet of the few passers by. This was a distraction from the noises.

From an adjacent cell came screams and cries of pain. It sounded like someone being tortured. Reaching out with her mind, Sister Lam soon realised that it was a recording. She was not impressed with this cheap trick but reflected that it was better than having someone tortured in the next cell for her benefit.

After a few hours alone, Quin came in with a plate. His expression was almost apologetic as he laid down the empty plate. "You will be fed when you talk."

He was surprised at the response. Sister Lam laughed
"Well I need to lose some weight."

Quin looked, or perhaps leered, at her naked body as if assessing whether she needed to or not. She had seen plenty of outré male fantasies in the minds of the uncles and she was married to Xavier so she thought herself unshockable. Quin's fantasies were definitely off the Richter Scale for disgustingness however.

And suddenly Sister Lam noticed something else in his mind. It was his job to get her to talk and normally one he enjoyed but if she did talk he was honour-bound to silence her by killing her if necessary. He was a follower of Saint Miranda.

Extract from the diary of Septimus Quin

(*This diary was found some years after the events recorded here. It was in an erased and encrypted file which Xavier eventually decoded. Septimus Quin was not from a family of seven. His father just rather liked the sound of "Septimus" - Narrator*)

Brand has been called away on urgent business for The Dictator and left the Sister Lam case for me. She would normally have given me a run-down on the prisoner's "buttons" but she gave me no such information on Sister Lam.

Many years ago, according to legend it was in Salzburg, the Torturer's Guild was founded by a highly successful torturer whose name has not come down to us. This is all right and proper. I do not confide my name, or at least my Christian name, to anyone except this secret diary.

Brand of course is not entitled to join this most secret of secret societies because she is a woman. I confess she is a fair torturer. For a woman. But the rules come down from antiquity. What also comes down is the Torturer's Manual. Allegedly written by our legendary leader, known only as X. It has been expanded and elaborated over the years.

By the manual my treatment of Sister Lam should have been most effective. Starvation is a tried and tested method. Torture by thirst is quicker but there have been too many accidental deaths from it to make it an effective torture. Many prisoners end up drinking unsuitable fluids and dying. Most unprofessional.

Sister Lam has so far survived ninety days naked in a freezing cold cell with nothing to eat and she has not only survived but actually refused drink too. When I see her and try to tempt a confession with food she just talks about recipes. I am beginning to think Brand's "urgent business" was just a way to land me with this failure of a torturee.

I tried out, one after another, the suggestions in the manual. How on earth can I get someone to confess by the risky business of torture by drowning when she just holds her breath, apparently indefinitely? And she is impervious to physical pain it seems.

I have bombarded the cell with appalling music, loud enough to make your eardrums bleed. All she does is talk about something called "Oasis".

There is one thing the manual expressly forbids but I have done it a few times. Since my wife died I have made use of female prisoners for sex. They can hardly complain that it is unprofessional after all. Desperate situations call for desperate measures.

I am resolved that this is what I will do. I have never had such an attractive prisoner before so the idea is quite exciting. I will just have to silence my inner professional.

If I succeed in breaking her then I will have to deal with the fact that Miranda herself has ordered this prisoner killed if she provides any information about the sisters of Saint Miranda or Father Alon. Still one problem at a time.

Two torturers

For Sister Lam the only entertainment, apart from the visits of Quin, was watching the window. Boots marched past. Sometimes singly, sometimes in squads. She counted the number of steps it took to clear her small field of vision. She made up stories about the people who were marching past. She noted the intensity of the shine and the state of repair of the boots. However it is true that boots can eventually become tedious.

And one day there was a limousine. A pair of boots came smartly round to the passenger door and then a pair of the most elegant high heels supporting nicely turned ankles in what she imagined were the latest style in nylons emerged.

She jumped to the conclusion that this was one of the Mirandas and in the split second she was in sight, Sister Lam shouted the first thing that came to her mind.

"Thank you for the sugar!"

She hoped this was either a code phrase or at least sufficiently weird to gain Miranda's attention.

She was rewarded with the vision of Miranda actually kneeling down in the dust, heedless of her nylons, to peer into the little window. There was a smile and Miranda mouthed something. Sister Lam was not much cop at lip-reading but she thought it might have been "I know." However she soon had something else to occupy her.

In her cell she had been naked for so long it seemed perfectly natural. When Quin came in however **he** was stark naked and it was immediately apparent what he had come for. The bed, she imagined, was very uncomfortable although she could not feel it. The psychological effect of being at such close quarters with Quin was the closest to torture she would ever come.

She was pushed onto the bed and Quin, amazed by the lack of resistance, parted her legs. She knew that having sex here would keep her in this place forever. She smiled and turned over so she was face downwards on the bed. Once again Quin was amazed at her calm strength.

His amazement was to turn to astonishment. Suddenly

Sister Lam could feel – actually feel – hands tightening around her neck. We can only imagine the consternation of Quin as he found himself trying to rape the bed. His prisoner had vanished.

The shock had caused Tilly to awake and her astral projection was no more. She found herself back in the pentacle in Professor Hollands' house. She was staring into the livid face of Kaspar who was making a strenuous effort to strangle her.

Kaspar was strong and Tilly's normal body had none of the strength of her astral projection which all came from her imagination. She struggled ferociously but all she did was succeed in knocking over a metal censer. The clatter of the censer distracted Kaspar for a split second.

"Now if I can just whack the brute over the head with the bloody thing. Sod it, it's rolled too far away."

Kaspar's pressure on her windpipe was relentless and she felt her consciousness going away. She thought that her last thought ought to be an appeal to Saint Katherine or ideally she should forgive Kaspar so that her own sins might be forgiven.

"You fucking bastard, I hope you rot in hell." was as close as she got.

She was gone. And without any transition she was in a comfortable boudoir with blue silk drapes and matching furnishings. She herself was dressed in a lovely blue silk robe. She recognised the place immediately.

"Well you haven't died and this isn't heaven." came an amused voice Tilly knew and loved.

"Doctor Katherine!"

The two women embraced. Tilly looked round the room and Doctor Katherine caught her thought. "How come I end up here but Xavier ends up in a dreary graveyard."

"Well you are lucky. You will have seen that Xavier started out with Wolf-Dietrich as his spiritual mentor but what about now? I would have said the roles were more evenly balanced and in the end Xavier could be helping Wolf-Dietrich more than the other way round.

"And what do you want to do to Garcia?" As she aimed this unexpected question, Tilly was reminded that she had no secrets from Doctor Katherine. It was useless to hide anything and in her heart she didn't want to.

"I wanted"

Doctor Katherine gave her a look.

"I want to kill him. I want to save those people he poisoned in St Michael's. I don't want to create a temporal paradox. I just want to save them."

Doctor Katherine sat quietly for a moment and Tilly caught the thought directly from her mentor. If she killed Garcia, Wolfie would be lost to the cause. This evil deed had had unintended consequences and as for Miranda...

Doctor Katherine was as ever reluctant to give Tilly information about the future but the information was clear in her mind. There **was** a Saint Miranda. It was just that she hadn't yet been called into existence. That was as far as Doctor Katherine could afford to go. Somehow Garcia was instrumental in Miranda's role.

"What will you do about Kaspar?"

Tilly hesitated and as she did so all her aggressive feelings towards Kaspar came under control. She had a whole lot of things she wanted to do to Kaspar. As she considered them one by one, Doctor Katherine smiled patiently at some and with genuine amusement at others until eventually Tilly realised she wanted to forgive him.

"I know a rogue Methodist who always says that forgiving your enemies is the best way to seriously piss them off." She tried, too late, to change "piss them off" into a phrase Doctor Katherine would find acceptable. Having your mind read is uncomfortable if you need to censor your words in any way.

"Yes it is." Doctor Katherine smiled and they talked of other things. Tilly never revealed what they discussed but several hours passed. In "real life" only about a minute had elapsed before Tilly choked, coughed and spluttered awake. She was back chez Hollands.

A very pleased Geert Hollands was standing astride a very unconscious Kaspar. She was swinging the censer nonchalantly. Kaspar was bleeding profusely from a cut in the back of his head.

"He's going to bleed to death."

"How very unfortunate." Geert said insincerely, "How about 'Thank you for saving my life' and 'Shouldn't I get some clothes on?' young Tilly?"

Tilly pulled on her jeans and t-shirt while Geert gave Kaspar an unnecessary kick and found herself a chair to sit in. From the chair she watched with disbelief as Tilly tried to stop Kaspar from bleeding.

"Why the Hell are you helping that piece of shit? He was just trying to kill you wasn't he? Or was it all some kinky game? I can remember when Terrence..."

Tilly cut short this line of thought before it got out of hand. She grasped at the only explanation Geert was likely to accept.

"Dead men can't talk, Geert. And I happen to know a qualified torturer."

"Oh really, who's that then?"

"Xavier."

Geert looked at her daughter-in-law with an amused pity.

"Tilly, Tilly, Tilly when are you going to realise that half of what Xavier says is apocryphal and the other half is just bollocks?"

"I'm going to ring him just the same. Do you fancy tying this piece of shit to a chair for me?"

The two women hauled the dead weight of the more-or-less still living Kaspar into a chair and Geert went to the task of tying him up with an excess of enthusiasm.

Tilly phoned Xavier.

"Well when is he going to be here? I have to cook dinner you know."

Geert's peevish complaint was interrupted when Xavier literally materialised behind her and gave her a perfunctory peck on the cheek. She went off in a fine old huff to marinade the vegetables.

When she came back the two of them were waiting for Kaspar to recover from Geert's blow to his head. She tried to help by slapping his face a few times then vanished off to the kitchen again. She returned with extra long matches. With a sort of grim amusement she adjusted his clothing and set fire to his pubic hairs. It certainly got Kaspar's attention and he was fully awake.

"You can thank me later." was her parting shot.

Tilly poured lemonade over the affected area.

"You bloody bitch." was all they could get out of him for a while. When he had calmed down a bit, Tilly said, "I want you to know that I forgive you."

"What?"

"I want you to know that I forgive you."

"You people are weak. The dictator is strong. You do not stand a chance." There was nothing of the old Kaspar. It was a voice without feeling.

"And yet you are the one tied to the chair."

"That was thanks to Geert. She isn't weak."

Xavier had a vivid image of Geert that he really could have done without. It told him in way too much detail what Geert, or her astral projection, had been getting up to with Kaspar. Then he saw a vivid image of Tilly lying naked on the floor and Kaspar's thoughts as he was strangling her. He didn't seem to want forgiveness.

"So you work for the dictator."

"No shit, Sherlock!"

"Miranda." No response

"Ygael."

Xavier sensed the ambiguity. In the world of intelligence sides shifted. The resistance penetrated security. Security infiltrated the resistance.

Xavier concluded "Oh I see. Ygael wants to kill the Dictator but then he wants to take his place. Your duty is to stop him but if he succeeds you would just as cheerfully work for him?"

"Well a job is a job." If Kaspar was surprised that Xavier knew so much of his hidden thoughts, he didn't show it.

"Oh but this hasn't always been your job." Xavier could see Kaspar at the wheel of a limousine. He was joking with the three children in the back. They were apprehensive about going to a new school and he was telling them it was going to be fine. Then the teachers welcomed them and took them into the school. The kindly teachers were talking enthusiastically about all the fun the children were going to have there. They gave them each a drink. One chose milk and two chose coke.

The drinks were drugged. Kaspar had been struck by the unnecessary cruelty. The drink was only drugged not poisoned because the Dictator insisted that they could only be incinerated alive. Incredibly he had a prejudice against illegal cremations. This was not a cremation. It was an execution.

Kaspar had to make sure that orders were carried out to the letter.

"So after the killing of the children you became a journalist?"

This did pull up Kaspar short and he struggled to conceal his thoughts, eventually saying,

"I go where The Dictator sends me."

Xavier glimpsed some of Kaspar's "jobs." He was in a basement room assisting Petra and Neeta in beating up an old man. The old man was of no significance to the Dictator; just practice. Then he was in a luxury suite coldly instructing one of the Mirandas in The Dictator's sexual preferences. Later, he was driving in a Jeep with boisterous soldiers. They were running over the legs of children. The children were guilty, or at least accused, of throwing a stone at a convoy.

Then he saw an airfield. Kaspar was in a light aircraft landing at night. He was handed a false passport, money and documents.

"So you had to enter the country illegally to keep up the pretence that you are a rebel?"

Silence.

"At a small airport near Newbury? On a cold day in August?"

All of Xavier's victims reached a stage when they realised they might as well tell the truth. In Kaspar's case this took the form of a nod.

"Now you will tell me about the Mirandas."

Kaspar sneered. "There are six of them. They have enough brain cells to keep their bodies moving and feed themselves but little more. The Dictator does not require their brains."

"But there is an exception." Xavier prompted.

"The mother of the little whore."

"How do you know Jenny?" Tilly interjected.

Kaspar didn't answer her. Xavier had a picture of Kaspar and the under-age girl in the back of a taxi and again in a room with a flea-bitten bed. He looked at Tilly.

"Oh. As I thought."

"Are you going to kill me?"

"No. You have been very useful. We don't want you to stay in the country though. The police will be closing down the airbase near Newbury in twenty-four hours. You leave the country. You will be sought as an illegal entrant after the same period."

"Just one last thing." Tilly was annoyed at the lack of attention from Kaspar when he wasn't trying to kill her. "Thank you for the sugar?"

Kaspar actually smiled and they had a glimpse of the old,

affable Kaspar from Ye Olde Bore.

"Miranda, Jenny's Miranda, goes out into the poor areas of town and she leaves gifts for the poor. "Thank you for the sugar" is a password for the supporters of Miranda."

Geert returned to announce dinner was ready and Kaspar wasn't having any.

"No Kaspar has to go."

"Has he explained what he was doing with your wife?"

"Oh yes. He was trying to kill her."

Xavier just had to show off before Kaspar left them. He held the heavy metal censer. "One last thing. If you so much as look at Tilly again. " He crushed the heavy metal of the censer between his hands like paper, "you will find out just how soft we are."

Xavier popped home to change and they sat down to a delicious meal.

"Well I thought he was a wrong'un from the start." was Geert's summary of Kaspar

"A wrong'un?" teased Xavier, "not a ne'er-do-well or a hobbledehoy?" He was still recovering from his vivid images of Kaspar and Geert's astral projections engaging in sex games. Obviously what happened in dreams stayed in dreams for Geert.

"You may laugh. I think he was a spook." She produced the word with triumph. She had seen it on TV and been waiting to use it ever since.

"Well he was hardly a friendly ghost." Tilly had fully recovered from the attempted murder obviously. Perhaps forgiving him had helped.

Over the Cabernet Sauvignon they reverted to the issue of the opposition to the dictatorship. This was a side of things, Geert was less interested in but it did not stop her having an opinion.

"So you think because Ygael and his followers want death to the dictator, not the dictatorship, that can only mean they want to take his place? Have a new dictator?" she asked.

"Well," Xavier said slowly as he sought to gather his thoughts. "Ygael thinks the whole dictatorship will fall apart without the dictator and history suggests this is possible. Mussolini was replaced by someone whose name nobody remembers..."

"Badoglio." put in Geert.

"Well someone whose name most people don't remember and that was the end of that. On the other hand when Stalin kicked the bucket it did not lead to the end of Stalinism."

"Just Stalinism with a human fist." put in Tilly and got the beginning of a smile.

"What we do know for sure is that people close to the dictator like Kas..."

"No I certainly forget his name" Geert said dismissively

"people close to The Dictator think Ygael would like to be the next dictator and they would work for him quite happily."

"And the Mirandas?"

"They would have their throats cut. They would become a symbol of popular rebellion if they survived." Xavier was quite clear on that point, having read more of Kaspar's hidden thought than he knew.

Extract from the diary of Jenny

I had a hard day's night. That's a song isn't it? Well it was hard. The customers were drunk and smelly and took ages to finish their business and there were so few of them I was standing around on those ridiculous bloody heels for hours on end. When I finally went to the cafe, Sister Lam was back. Obviously old wassisname the owner of the cafe had done a deal with The Man to hold on to his top washer-up.

Anyway my bloody feet were killing me and I couldn't think of nothing else. Sister Lam noticed this right away and before I knew it she was washing my feet and massaging them while I had a cup of what passes for coffee. It was lovely. Obviously I don't mean the coffee!

And then Lucy came in and then Suki who wants us to call her Shelly now. And of course they wanted their feet washed too. In between washing the dishes and washing our feet, Sister Lam had a busy old night of it. She still found time to talk to me really quiet like. "I have seen Miranda – I have seen your mother. She gave me a message but I can't make head nor tail of it. She said, well she mouthed the words, there were armed guards, 'I know' was what she said."

Well I will have to think about that. But first I will have to sleep so goodnight, diary.

The Watchtower

Wolfie, Xavier and Sister Lam gathered in the gloom of St Miranda's church. They had no need to talk out loud and given the interest which Neeta and Petra had taken in the Church they regarded it as politic to share their thoughts silently. We can eavesdrop though.

"I fail to understand why you are spending so much of your time with those street girls." Wolfie did not make much effort to conceal the fact that for him the word "spending" meant "wasting".

"They are most worthwhile in their own right. My work with them is the most useful work I have done. And even you might be interested in the Miranda connection."

Xavier held her hand, then thought that was patronising. Then Sister Lam thought that's OK and he thought, "Well it takes your mind off killing Garcia." She took her hand out of his sharpish. Try having a telepathic lover sometime, it is less fun than you might think.

She smiled ruefully and attended to Wolfie who was framing a question, "What about the Watchtower?"

"Jehovah's Witnesses?"

Wolfie wondered, half to himself, whether Sister Lam would ever learn when levity was inappropriate and he concluded she probably wouldn't.

"I have caught distinct images. So have you," he looked at Xavier. "A place called The Watchtower. It is associated in Ygael's mind with some forthcoming event which seems to trouble him. Xavier you are better at this than I am, what have you picked up?"

Xavier liked being flattered and always sought to justify Wolfie's confidence when he received it. "An abandoned building on a hill. They call it the Watchtower and there is something about its past which is important as well as its future. It is well off the beaten track so I think it could be a place to meet away from prying eyes. Or as far away as anywhere in the Dictatorship is from prying eyes. So it is likely that some important meeting involving a number of people is coming up and this is the proposed venue."

"I've seen it too." Sister Lam added, "It is only vague but at least one of the Sisters of Miranda had this image, a wild place in the moonlight and a gathering. Presumably a gathering of the resistance. An attempt to bring the two wings together for some purpose. Though why the Sisters are involved I do not know."

"So spend time finding out. These guttersnipes of yours might be useful...there is no need to bridle every time I use the word guttersnipes I mean no offence by it. They might, they just might, come up with some information although my torturer here informs me that whores (stop bridling, Sister.

Now) are never great sources of information because they are only anxious to get on to the next client. The only factor in their favour is that men sometimes say things in front of them because they do not look on them as human."

He looked Sister Lam in the eye as he added, "which I do, whatever I might think of them."

...

So it was that three nights later, the three found themselves approaching The Watchtower on a moonless night. There were the Sisters of Miranda. They were dressed in grey cloaks and all wore hoods. There were also two groups of about eighty men who had affected balaclavas and face masks to conceal their identity.

Sister Lam imitated the sisters of Miranda. It struck her that by concealing their identity from any ill-wishers they had also concealed their identity from each other so this diminished the chance she would be exposed. Xavier wore a hoodie and a scarf concealed half his face. It was a cold night anyway. Wolfie had years of practice on the astral plane and he could pass unseen whenever he wanted to.

They were using no sound equipment. Xavier launched into an explanation of how sound equipment could be eavesdropped remotely and the others shushed him, although he had said nothing aloud.

The speaker was one of the striking miners from the northern province. He talked about the hardships the miners endured, the ruthless behaviour of the military and the miners' spirit of resistance.

As he was speaking Xavier was trying to read the reactions.

Ygael and his faction were trying to listen politely but if anything they looked bored and impatient. These popular struggles were nothing to do with the serious business of killing the Dictator and that was all they wanted to discuss.

The Sisters of Miranda listened in silence. That seemed to be their role in this meeting as far as could be ascertained. They also serve who only stand and wait in the freezing cold. And one rather surprising thought which Xavier caught from some of them was "If you want someone to kill The Dictator then we know someone who can."

And the other faction of the resistance (or the true resistance as they styled themselves) were all behind the miners. It was they who had insisted on involving the striking miners in the first place. It did not fit Ygael's idea of a secret conspiracy.

As the discussion developed it became apparent that both factions were more concerned with scoring points off each other than with killing the Dictator or overthrowing the dictatorship.

"So they are the people's front." Xavier gestured towards Ygael's faction.

"And they are the popular front" rejoined Sister Lam.

Then they had to explain the joke to Wolfie who concluded,

"This is another example of that democracy business you keep babbling on about. It would be laughable if it didn't mean the dictator could get away with murder."

They attended to the thoughts of the Sisters of Miranda. Most of them were trying to absent themselves from the squabbling and focus on the image of Miranda. Wolfie nodded towards one of the sisters and the others attended to her thoughts. They were very different indeed. This sister was thinking about Miranda indeed but she was thinking about murdering her.

Sister Lam realised two things simultaneously. This was Captain Brand. *And this vision of killing Miranda was not a bit of wishful thinking. It was a memory.*

Captain Brand was immediately aware of Sister Lam and Xavier converging on her and she sought to make her escape through an open portal in a ruined wall. As she did so she was suddenly aware of the imposing figure of Wolfie apparently blocking her exit. She had no reason to know she could have walked straight through him so Xavier and Sister Lam were able to capture her easily.

They were so intent on their captive they momentarily took their eyes off the rally. Things were getting ugly between the two factions. One got the impression they always did. As they questioned Captain Brand fighting had broken out.

Sister Lam drew their attention to what was happening. The Sisters of Miranda were quietly interposing their bodies between the combatants. "Stupid Whores," was Captain Brand's only thought.

"This is your democratic process is it?" was Wolfie's amused remark to Sister Lam.

Sister Lam just noted that what the Sisters were doing was working. It was stopping the opposition tearing from itself apart. Still it was unlikely that there would be any more rational discussion between the factions that night so they paid their full attention to Captain Brand.

In her mind there was a lively apprehension that she was about to be tortured. She started to talk. The trio shared the thought that she was trying to divert attention from the fact she had killed one of the Mirandas.

"The opposition are meeting here because of the history of the Watchtower. The Dictator does not believe in history. After all history can be falsified and as for historians..." she drew her finger across her throat.

"The history, or more likely the legend, of the Watchtower is at least a hundred years old. It talks of a time when the Dictatorship had no Dictator. This is obviously absurd but that does not stop the common scum believing in it. They believe the country had a King in those days. Fanciful and more appropriate for a fairy story really.

"The poor were starving. The harvest had failed two years running (some stories say three – so much for history) And there was discontent. A tax collector was driven out of the local village minus his trousers for example. Soldiers from the Watchtower were sent into the village to pacify them and a number of them ended up nice and peaceful in the graveyard."

Captain Brand laughed. She made an unpleasant sound with no humour in it.

"And then a man in the village, some say his name was Ananias, rallied the men in the village square. Ananias harangued them for about an hour. He told them the poor were poor because the rich were rich and all that sort of nonsense. He agitated them to such a pitch that they resolved the march on the Watchtower. They had torches, cudgels and two ancient guns somebody had been keeping in their loft. They shouldn't have stood a chance.

"The King had very foolishly recruited his soldiers locally. Instead of opening fire on the mob they listened as Ananias started haranguing them. He was obviously a first class haranguer because he persuaded the garrison to come over to the rebels. Pausing only to shoot an officer the men hated already they raised the red flag over the Watchtower and began to prepare to seize power.

"The king had his answer of course. He brought in foreign mercenaries and there was a bloody massacre on this spot. So it is a bit ironic that the revolting scum should choose to gather here."

Captain Brand warmed to her tale and Sister Lam brought the matter straight back to the present by casually asking "You tortured Miranda to death?"

Captain Brand tried to bluster but Sister Lam brought out more and more of the details she had seen in Captain Brand's mind while the Captain had been trying to distract their attention with the history lesson.

"You cut off her hair. Then you cut off her fingers. Do I have to go on. You punched her in the face repeatedly then made her look in a mirror."

"You were only ordered to kill her though." was Xavier's final point.

"Well yes but you must allow me to use my own particular methods."

"The Dictator agreed with that?"

"Once the order had been given the Dictator just wanted it carried out by any means."

"And this was eight, excuse me, ten years ago?" was Wolfie's contribution.

Captain Brand had given up wondering how on earth they knew that. Kaspar had reported on The Mirror of Eternity but Brand had assumed Xavier was a fantasist.

"A fantasist and a technologist." Xavier corrected her unspoken thought. "Anyway you needn't worry. Sister Lam won't be probing your buttons today. You have a long walk home though because we are borrowing your car."

Extract from the Diary of Captain Brand

Bloody hellfire and damnation! Those incompetent idiots

Neeta and Petra will pay for this. First that randy pervert Quin let Sister Lam escape. He paid for that with his head of course. Eventually he paid with his head. First he paid with other bits of his anatomy. The torturer tortured – that would make a good film.

Then Neeta and Petra were so useless in infiltrating the sisters of Miranda I had to take the job on myself. I don't want to spend my bloody time with those smelly whores. They disgust me.

I don't question anything the Dictator decides but he is too soft-hearted with the people. Somehow Miranda always talks him out of wiping the stupid bitches out. It is up to me to save him from himself. We could have just bombed the bloody watchtower tonight. Instead I went to gather information. And now I have to sit down and write a report pretending I have some information when I am running on empty.

Then Neeta and Petra are in for a beating. A good hard one.

Jenny visits St Miranda's

"I have no idea how you persuaded the Doctor to let me come with you, Sister Lam."

"To be honest with you, Jenny, I don't think he quite knows either. I think it was mainly because he was tired and he wanted a night off so he gave you one."

"Sister Lam, it's about the Doctor. He's good looking isn't

he."

"I am not an expert." Sister Lam said diplomatically, burying deeply her inappropriate revulsion for the Doctor.

"Yeah well that's as may be but you have got eyes though."

"Mm"

"Well, I want to ask you something."

The something was screaming in Jenny's mind but Sister Lam endured the slow unfolding of the embarrassed question until eventually Jenny said aloud and very quickly so the words would get out before she thought better of them. "Do you think he loves me?"

"Well what do you think? You know him better than I do."

"Do you always answer a question with a question?"

"Why do you ask?" They said in unison and laughed.

"Well he says he does but when we have … you know... it's not really different from having it with a client and I hate all of them. It should be different, surely I should feel something different. But I don't. Perhaps it's me.

" After all he has been very good to me and I do owe him all this money but he can be so cruel at times too. I don't like being called a 'cash cow'. I mean he says it with a laugh but it isn't that funny. But then he has those lovely eyes and when he smiles I know I love him so perhaps that is enough."

"Well Maria, Jenny – which is your name by the way?"

"Well neither of those but then your name isn't Sister Lam either is it?"

"Well Jenny then, I think you can see the good in him which a lot of people can't." That was as far as Sister Lam wanted to go on this topic tonight.

"Well this is the place."

Jenny looked up at the imposing Baroque façade of St Miranda's. She was dressed as usual in black tights and a flimsy blouse but this was concealed under a coat Sister Lam provided for her.

"Well you wouldn't feel comfortable in church would you. It doesn't matter to me or to God what you wear but I want you to feel comfortable too."

"I am not sure I feel comfortable as it is. This is nothing like the Church back home. What is it, a cathedral or summat?"

"No it is just a rather posh church but the sisters of Miranda are not all posh by any means. You might like to lose the gum before we go in though don't you think?"

Inside the church was brightly lit and the altar to St Miranda was glowing with hundreds of devotional candles. For the first time in years, Jenny dipped her fingers in the holy water and made the sign of the cross. She seemed surprised the holy water didn't burn her. Sister Lam whispered, "You have as much right to be here as anybody. Promise me you will remember that."

Jenny smiled at her.

Half a dozen Sisters of Miranda were already there and they all hugged Jenny in a deliberate gesture of acceptance.

They knew of Sister Lam's work with the street girls and in principle they approved. They had to overcome a deep-seated prejudice against the girls though.

"It is very good to see a Magdalene like you in the church."

"The name's Jenny. Why are they laughing?" The last question was addressed to Sister Lam.

"Well they were saying you are like Saint Mary Magdalene. They are trying to be nice in their own way."

Sister Lam could detect that Jenny was about to respond and she quietly advised her, "We don't want to swear in church."

Jenny simmered down.

Soon about a hundred women were crowded into the church. Sister Lam scanned the faces for Neeta, Petra or Captain Brand. She couldn't know that Neeta and Petra were being punished brutally by Captain Brand. It was to toughen them up.

"Saint Miranda, sister of our sorrows and guardian of our fate. We ask your blessing on Jenny in the awful life she leads." You didn't need to be a mind-reader to know that the woman speaking had nothing but repugnance for Jenny and the other street girls but she wanted to do the right thing in the presence of the saint and before her sisters.

"Saint Miranda, we beg you to hear our prayer." The other women responded.

As the service continued, Sister Lam focussed on the

women in the church who were wearing mantillas, there were about a dozen of them in all. She tried to read anything suspicious in their thoughts.

There was one woman who had come in quite late and was keeping in the shadows. With a shock Sister Lam realised that this woman was the Miranda she had seen very briefly during her imprisonment. Miranda's mind was in turmoil. She had thought Jenny was safe at home in the village. She had just heard that she was living an "awful life" and her mind was full of speculations about what that might mean.

Miranda made no move and Sister Lam had to keep her own counsel because to reveal the presence of Miranda in the church would have triggered a panic among the sisters. She also knew that leaving Jenny alone would be unwise. The sisters were at best ambiguous towards her and very uneasy in her presence as if prostitution were catching.

Sister Lam could see in some minds the thought that the street girls were a temptation to their husbands and boyfriends. One woman was burning with resentment about the money she thought (actually she was quite certain in her own mind) that her husband was spending on prostitutes when the family had to do without.

Sister Lam could tell that Miranda's mind was in conflict. She wanted to slip away before the end of the service to avoid discovery but she was driven to make contact with her daughter. Miranda was sitting between two pillars against the back wall of the church.

As the service was ending, Sister Lam moved swiftly towards her and took Jenny by the hand. The pair turned to face the congregation, effectively screening Miranda from the other women.

"Why did you bring me here? I could tell those stuck-up bitches hated me like poison."

"A bit quieter perhaps. I am sure that was true of some of them. Some of them wanted to be sympathetic or at least thought they ought to. But I brought you here to meet one special person. Let's wait until they have dispersed. Let's wait just here.

"Tell me what you remember about your mother."

She could tell she had Miranda's undivided attention now so she was unlikely to leave just yet.

"I remember everything about her." said Jenny fiercely.

"What I mean is, I don't know about her and I would like to."

After a while Jenny started to talk.

"She used to read me stories. The books were a load of cheap old rubbish but as I got older I could tell she was just using the characters from the books to make up stories about them herself. She was clever like that. That was the happiest time.

"She fed me of course, whenever it was possible to buy food. My dad drank a fair amount of his wages but like he said , 'I earn the money. I decide what to spend it on.' And he could be a bit rough and ready when he had had enough of the firewater. She was probably the worst cook in the dictatorship; my aunt Francesca was a hundred times better at cooking and she used to take the piss out of her cooking something chronic.

"I just miss her. I miss her good tempers and her bad tempers. I even miss the dreadful cooking if you can believe it."

"That is quite enough about my cooking!" Miranda had had enough. Jenny actually shrieked when she heard her mother's voice and both of the women shushed her until she subsided.

Miranda was used to taking charge. She was certainly used to taking charge of Jenny, "Listen. I know somewhere we can go and talk. Come with me."

Miranda the assassin

"I would like Sister Lam to come with me."

"Ah Sister Lam. I remember seeing you in prison very briefly. And of course we have all heard about the good work you have been doing with the...WHAT THE FUCK. Jenny you haven't been...

"That was the 'terrible life' those sunkets were talking about..."

"Well I didn't know. I thought it was some illness or..."

Lost for explanations, Miranda put her arms around Jenny as if she could take away all the hurt through her skin just as she had done when Jenny was a child. And Sister Lam could tell it was beginning to work.

Miranda wordlessly included Sister Lam in the invitation when she took Jenny by the hand and led her out of the church.

A few streets from the church there was a run-down apartment building. The concrete was stained and cracked and the stairway smelt of urine and worse. Sister Lam noticed three men lounging casually and smoking cigarettes.

Miranda saw her looking and explained, "The Secret Police have to keep an eye on me but these guys are loyal to me. I have had to rely on them to put in false reports to Captain Brand when necessary."

The apartment itself however was as luxurious as the block was squalid, as befitted the consort of The Dictator.

Miranda explained, "Poverty on the outside, wealth on the inside. It is a guard against the envy of the poor and the designs of thieves. One of The Dictator's sayings."

"Jenny, you're hungry." Miranda went to the largest Smeg fridge-freezer imaginable. "There are a variety of microwave meals in here. Just pick anything you like. And you can put it in the microwave yourself if you distrust my cooking. And then you can tell me. Well you can tell me as many details as you think I ought to hear about what has been going on.

Jenny took off her coat and ignored the way her mother

was looking at her clothes. Her attitude said that Miranda would have to get used to them.

Miranda turned to Sister Lam while Jenny was wolfing down the lasagne.

"Kaspar used to boast, do you know Kaspar?"

Sister Lam's hand had gone instinctively to her throat but of course her astral projection did not have the marks of Kaspar's attentions. She just nodded.

"Well Kaspar went out of his way to make himself the living expert on the street girls and he left out no details when he made reports about his nocturnal visits. I understand he claimed expenses too. I know enough to know it is a terrible life."

"Like yours?" Jenny's remark was like a slap across the face to Miranda. She wasn't a prostitute...and then she remembered her training to satisfy The Dictator's little foibles in the bedroom and she wondered.

"I have enough to eat." She said lamely.

Jenny actually laughed. "You're right, mum. And look at this lovely place with its freezer and microwave. I am fuc...damned if I know how to use a f..microwave anyway. And it's warm. So warm. You don't know how cold it is on the street at night.

"I do have a lover who protects me though and he's a doctor.

"I have someone who protects me and he's The Dictator."

Sister Lam was suddenly still. She could see vividly what

was in Miranda's mind. She was going to kill The Dictator.

Mother and daughter went on talking and Sister Lam tried to rationalise the vision she had had of Miranda killing the Dictator. After all, it might be because Miranda had to kill the Dictator before he killed her as an inconvenience.

In the conversation, Jenny harped on about how the Doctor loved and protected her. It was as if she wanted Miranda to think she was safe, despite the 'terrible life' and perhaps feel a bit less guilty about leaving her behind in the first place.

Miranda was having none of it. The Doctor was going to be paid off and Jenny could come and live in this apartment, "so that I can feed you up a bit. You're nothing but skin and bone."

"Nobody could say that about you." Jenny gibed and Miranda was on the point of rebuking her when she laughed instead.

Suddenly serious again she made the arrangements. Jenny was not going to go back to the Doctor with the money.

"If he thinks you have a rich relative then he will just hold you to ransom. It would be easy money. I am going to have to entrust this job to Sister Lam. Don't fail me."

She didn't stop to wonder why she suddenly trusted Sister Lam so completely.

Second appointment with the Doctor

Sister Lam had no difficulty getting the Doctor's address from Charles, the cafe owner. Charles made it his business to know everything.

Another block of flats no different in kind from the one Miranda occupied except the loungers were not secret police, they were just loungers. And, when he eventually answered her knocking, the Doctor's flat was a pigsty.

"Oh I am sorry, Sister, the cleaners have a day off today."

"Or a year off this year."

"Have it your own way. Where is that stupid little whore?"

"I have come to you about Jenny."

"You want to take her place, Sister? I am surprised at you. You are a bit old for my clients but I will give you a try-out on the bed here if you like."

"Jenny's mother has come to take her back to the village."

"Like fuck she has. She stays or goes when I say so."

"Well you are going to say so."

"Why on earth should I do that?"

Sister Lam made no reply. She calmly took a wad of notes and left them on the table.

"That is nowhere near enough to pay off her debt."

"We both know the debt is whatever you want it to be. Choose for it to be this. It is a lot of money."

The Doctor reached for the cash and Sister Lam's hand came down on his wrist like steel handcuffs. He was pinned to the table. She calmly held him there until he stopped struggling and realised that he would only be released when she chose to let him go.

"OK sister, you drive a hard bargain. Have a little drink with me before you go out into this cold night."

"Coke and Rohypnol? Not for me thanks."

"How do you know..."

"That is what you gave Jenny? Call it an educated guess, Doctor."

"You walked through these streets with all that money?"

"And me a weak and feeble woman?"

The Doctor looked at the darkening bruises on his wrists and smiled.

"Well get home safely, Sister."

Back at the cafe, Sister Lam was besieged with questions from the other girls. "back home to the village" was the cover story and she stuck to it. Other girls wanted her to contact their parents. This was the first time this had happened and she took on the work with gratitude. There had to be some compensation for dealing with people like the Doctor who were difficult to love.

The next time Sister Lam saw the Doctor he had a new girl in tow. The needle marks on her arms and the look in her eyes indicated that he had resorted to using heroin with this one. Her name was Lynda or occasionally Morganna.

Suki's story

Suki did not come from a village. Her mother was – last she knew – living in Capital City with a man who knocked her black and blue on a Saturday night and spent Sundays apologising. "A good man" as Suki called him. In her mind he was a good man because he stayed. If he left, Della, her mother, would have nothing. All she wanted to know was whether he had stayed or not. Sister Lam could see there was something more to this but didn't probe too deeply.

Standing at the door of Della's last known address, Sister Lam was suddenly aware that she didn't know what Shelly/Sheila/Suki's real name was. It was probably in there somewhere. Jenny had learned the best place to hide a real name was in a pile of false ones. Suki might be the same. People were reluctant to give out their full names in The Dictatorship and you called them by whatever they chose to call themselves.

"I am looking for Della."

"Nobody of that name here," The woman slammed the door. She happened to slam it on Sister Lam's fingers. Sister Lam didn't move a muscle. The woman looked in amazement at her apparently unbroken fingers and then at her face. She coughed comprehensively as if she had been smoking all night and focussed bloodshot eyes on Sister Lam.

"Supposing there was a Della. Supposing there had been a Della. What has it to do with you?"

Della's mind was a bit foggy but it didn't tax Sister Lam to realise that she was Della and she didn't want any trouble. There is an "I don't want any trouble" you could read in people's shoulders and in their eyes in The Dictatorship. Very few people avoided it. Even the uncles with their gangsta swagger had a fair touch of it.

"Well the Della I'm looking for has a daughter called, I think Suki... no Suzie," she corrected from Della's thoughts. "And I think she wants to get in touch."

"You get out of here." Della shouted with self-righteous rage, "Suzie – she ain't no Suki for heaven's sake – is staying with her uncle Mitch and she is just fine there. Now get on about your business or I will have those fingers off whatever it takes."

"She just wants to know if you're all right, Della."

"Well who the Hell are you?"

"Sister Lam."

"Well, Sister Lam, you shouldn't go poking your nose in matters which do not concern you. She is quite all right with her uncle Mitch to look after her."

"Do you know what Mitch is getting her to do?"

"What do you mean?"

"Do you know how she spends her time?" Sister Lam said carefully.

With an exasperated look, Della invited Sister Lam inside.

Sister Lam could not smell the overwhelming aroma of cannabis in the one-room flat but the overflowing ashtray and the roaches told their own story.

"Yes I know how she spends her time as you put it. Mitch was my uncle once upon a time right up until there was a condom-astrophe and I wound up pregnant with Suzie. It is a fact that Mitch had never beaten me up until then. He'd just kept me supplied with weed to keep me nice and mellow for the customers. One customer, one joint was the deal.

"When he found I was pregnant he was annoyed and he laid into me with his fists. It was only my prayers to Saint Miranda that spared me and spared my little Suzie.

"Now Suzie is out of the way, I can have clients back here. The only trouble is," she gave a self-deprecating laugh, "I am way too old."

"You are thirty four." Sister Lam read minds by second nature now and sometimes she forgot what people had told her out loud and what they had told her silently.

Della frowned for a moment but she wasn't a great one for concentrating and soon forgot what she was frowning about.

"I am way too old for the tourists. The tourists come here to get under-age sex which is illegal at home and they pay a lot better than the locals, the uncles make sure of that. So sister, are you shocked at my way of life?"

"Not really. I just came to find out that you are alive and well and to ask if there is anything you need."

"You're not going to lecture me then."

"I am not going to lecture anybody."

"There is nothing that I need. I am without a man. You know men usually need supporting rather than the other way round. So tell Suzie that I am OK. And thank you for coming."

And with that surprising last sentiment, Sister Lam went off to meet Miranda and Jenny

The fate of Kaspar
"Wolfie, Xavier, do you know a man called 'Kaspar'?"

Wolfie, Xavier, Sister Lam and Miranda were seated around her table. Jenny was glued to her mobile phone like any normal teenager. She had had to swear not to give out her location before Miranda relented and bought her one. Many of the girls had mobile phones but were supposed to use them for business calls only.

"You don't need to be a mind-reader, Sister Lam, why do I use that expression so often around you?"

Sister Lam smiled.

"You don't need to be a mind-reader to see that you do. However, Captain Brand, who you definitely know, came to me with a proposition. Kaspar had stolen or arranged to have someone steal, something Xavier would know a lot about. The mirror of eternity, Xavier, ring any bells?" She laughed good-naturedly at Xavier's discomfiture.

"This one was stolen from our office, not from the sealed room. Kaspar knew all about the sealed room. He claimed you had actually showed it to him. There are one or two ABCs of security which you might like to think about, Xavier. Having a sealed room where nobody can disturb you and then inviting one of the most dangerous of your enemies to have a look round is sort-of frowned on by security experts.

"Anyway Kaspar had it all set up in a room in the Dictator's compound. The pair of them took me to see it. I was given to understand that it only worked with the aid of some quite dangerous drugs. It turned out that the drugs were much too dangerous for either Brand or Kaspar to consider using them. Suddenly they both grabbed me and used a hypodermic syringe to inject me with what they thought were the correct drugs.

"I shouted a bit that this was no way to treat the Dictator's consort. They both laughed at that; I realised (without much of a shock, to be honest) that the Dictator had approved this course of action. They stressed that it was because the Dictator trusted my judgement that he wanted me to test this device. They also went on at length about the fact that I had in my youth experimented with a number of substances so they considered it to be safe. A bloody sight safer than trying it on themselves obviously.

"I waited the obligatory 45 minutes and Kaspar, who likes to lecture, explained the controls to me. The device would enable me to see the past and the future. Well it seemed like a load of baloney to me. I tried to out. I thought I would start by trying to look into my own past because I knew about that and likewise I sought to look at my own future.

"In the end I told them I couldn't see a damned thing. It's a fraud. I pushed the screen over and went to my own room to lie down for a bit.

"Of course, " Xavier said, "they would have got the drugs wrong so of course it wouldn't have worked."

"And the other possibility?" Miranda was openly laughing now. She looked round at all their faces as they all tried to read her mind. Her mind however was full of laughter and concealing her punchline.

"The other possibility is that I was lying. I did see my past, my childhood in the village. It made me sad."

"And the future?" Wolfie asked.

"Well let's deal with Kaspar's future first shall we? The Dictator thought it would be good for me to see how his story ended. I was called into The Dictator's office. It is a very austere room for a very austere man. There are no pictures on the walls, which are painted grey. There are no windows. There is a vast desk with a state-of-the art computer and only the one chair. Anyone who sees the Dictator does so standing.

"I was ushered in. Kaspar was ushered in. We came through a green door. There was also a red door. 'This Mirror of Eternity is a fraud. You have wasted a lot of time and money.' Kaspar made to speak, 'I do not require any comment from you. You may go. Use the red door.'

"Kaspar looked for a split-second as if he were going to disobey The Dictator but that was impossible for him. He turned and walked as if in a trance towards the red door which opened automatically. The Dictator pressed a button so that it remained open and indicated that I should watch. The corridor was identical to the one we had arrived by but after five yards it became tiled. Both the walls and the floor were white ceramic tiles. Kaspar took two steps onto the tiled area and two .22 bullets entered either side of his head and he slumped to the ground. As The Dictator closed the door I saw the sprinkler system come into operation, cleaning the blood off the tiles.

The Death of the Dictator

"I am very glad Sister Lam did not kill Garcia." said Miranda. "I saw in the Mirror of Eternity a number of stories which lead up to the death of The Dictator. I can tell you that if the sisters of Miranda were ever to have something so overtly political as a slogan, it will become "The Dictator will die" two weeks from now. I told Kaspar that I could see nothing in the Mirror of Eternity and indeed things were far from clear, Xavier. I must make that point. However I did have a very clear vision of how The Dictator will die. This fact will be reported to the sisters of Miranda as just that, 'a vision'. I do not want to involve any mention of Xavier's box of tricks. One thing I want you to do at your earliest convenience is to take it away with you."

Sister Lam could tell that Xavier was hurt to see his invention slighted, "We should be grateful to be able to return the Mirror even if it is at some unspecified date in the future after the demise of The Dictator." She announced, "You can see that it would be more powerful as a message to the Sisters of Miranda to describe it as 'a vision' than to try explaining The Mirror of Eternity to them. I imagine they take a dim view of some of the drugs which you use for example."

Xavier nodded and she turned to Miranda, "You have resisted all of our attempts to see into your thoughts and we quite understand this."

Wolfie did not look as if he understood anyone wanting to resist him in any way and a slight smile crossed Sister Lam's face. For some reason she thought this was amusing.

"Patriarchal!" was Wolfie's explosive response to Sister Lam, fortunately it was a silent response. "Patriarchal? I was a. Excuse me, Sister Lam, I **am** a Patriarch if you don't mind. In fact I am a Patriarch if you do mind. You let this democracy nonsense go to your head!"

Sister Lam smiled sweetly and then she focussed on Miranda. Miranda resisted mind-reading by keeping her mind full of laughter. "It is how I used to get through the bad times in my own life, Sister Lam." she said out loud,

"The less funny the situation, the more I would laugh about it. When my father…"

She paused for a moment then continued, "When my father used to do the things he did to me, I used to tease myself 'you are going to have a sore bottom in the morning,' and stuff like that. But Sister Lam, I will never forget that you brought my

Jenny back to me (Jenny looked up briefly when her name was mentioned but was back to texting in a trice) and I have decided that I am going to trust you. And I will take your friends, I mean your husband and your friend, on trust too.

Sister Lam had never dropped her cover enough to admit she was married to Xavier and she was impressed by this latest demonstration of Miranda's powers. Miranda's smile suggested both that she realised and that she intended to impress her.

Sitting around the table in the failing light, the three of them had a second-hand insight into Miranda's visions in The Mirror of Eternity.

Extract from the diary of Miranda

They have no smell! It is extraordinary. My mother taught me that you can tell a lot about somebody from their smell. The smell of their clothes tells the story of their outside life – their work and their home. The smell of the person tells you what is inside – how they feel, who they love. My mother taught me and she was never wrong. I remember when she teased the postmistress about her love for the garage mechanic. The postmistress was livid but she had to treat it all as a big joke. The villagers would have treated my mother as a witch were it not that she used her power to make jokes all the time. My best memories of her were of her surrounded by laughing women because she had revealed something about them which was naughty enough to cause laughter but not to blacken someone's character.

These three, Sister Lam, Xavier and the man they call Wolfie. They have no smell. Their clothes don't smell and they don't smell. It is enough to believe Kaspar's ravings about astral projections. After all the Mirror of Eternity was far-fetched enough and that proved to be true, up to a point.

Sister Lam under her nondescript clothes – a kind of anti-fashion statement – fits Kaspar's description of Tilly Hollands – brown-haired, brown-eyed, buxom barmaid. She is in her mid-thirties like Xavier. She is a mystery. She plays the role of a sister to perfection – abstaining from sex and from food completely and spending every waking hour helping the poor. Yet she has a powerful brain – it shows in everything she says and in her extraordinary mind-reading tricks; if they are tricks.

Xavier fits Kaspar's description – a fine mind concealed behind a lot of baloney. Geert's blue-eyed blond-haired mummy's boy. Withal he is incredibly strong according to Kaspar but I have no evidence of this.

I have left the strangest to last. The man they call Wolfie is apparently of an age with the other two but wields far more authority. His twenty-first century language and costume are things he does not seem comfortable with. The other two always position themselves so that nobody can touch him and he touches nobody else.

Everybody in The Dictatorship is familiar with Wolf-Dietrich

Von Raitenau after the TV series. I am aware that the series was commissioned by The Dictator who is a great admirer. Wolfie cannot be Wolf-Dietrich Von Raitenau because he seems terribly alive for someone who has been in the grave for four hundred years and I cannot imagine anybody calling him "Wolfie". I hardly like calling him that myself.

These are the people I am allowing into my mind. May Saint Miranda protect me.

The Procrastination Machine

"I have brought a package. It is for your eyes only."

The Revolutionary Committee liked to use the language of espionage, So Ygael was not surprised that Garcia was indulging in this piece of cloak-and-dagger mystique. He took the package and, following instructions, he made sure Garcia was out of the room before opening it. Garcia seemed pleased to leave.

He looked at the clock. It lacked thirty minutes of 2 pm and the meeting wasn't until 2.30 so he had time to examine it, whatever it was.

When he opened the padded envelope he found a grey book-sized device which appeared to have just a keyboard and no screen or printer.. The keyboard was strange. It was a random collection of letters and symbols. The alphabet was there but parts of it were repeated and there were circles, half-moons and stars.

Ygael typed in GCV. He smiled at his own slip and typed in CGV – the secret initials of the Revolutionary Committee. As soon as he typed that in, the Golden Wave began. It washed over Ygael and seemed to fill his consciousness. It unlocked feelings he had not felt in years. He took his hands off the keyboard to concentrate on the Golden Wave but it abruptly ceased.

He started typing again and the Golden Wave came back

stronger than ever. It was like the best sex he had ever had. It was like the best sex he had never had, to tell the truth. The Revolutionary Committee didn't leave a lot of time for that sort of thing.

He could see his problems. All the problems of his life were like small clouds and he could see and hear and feel as the Golden Wave was washing them all away. He was replete with food as he had never been in real life. He was drinking the finest wine and being seduced by the most beautiful women.

His typing became more and more frantic and the Golden Wave became stronger and stronger. He was in a film adventure. All his enemies were plotting against him but he could see their plans; he could read their very thoughts. He wiped them out with a wave of his hand. He watched them die in agony. The Dictator, Captain Brand, Miranda. They were all begging for mercy and he just laughed at them as he watched them all die.

2.30 came and went and still Ygael was typing furiously.

Previously

Captain Brand was sitting in her office. She was wearing black gloves and carefully putting what she called the Procrastination Machine into a padded envelope. By the end of the day she would be able to put Ygael's file into her "Dealt With" folder.

"Garcia," she said to the nervous courier, "you will deliver this parcel by 1.30 today or you will be wearing your testicles as earrings. I would like to say that it is a pleasure to have you on the team but since you have betrayed the Revolutionary Committee we will never be able to trust you either. You will be watched every step of the way.

After Garcia had gone about his business, she could not resist going down to the cells to take just one more look at the prisoner. The guard ushered her in proudly.

"This is Doctor Denisov, the man who invented the Procrastination Machine. It works, as you know Captain, by a psychotropic drug on the surface of the keyboard. We decided that the best way to test it out and to silence the inventor at the same time would be to use him as a guinea pig. After his hands had been placed on the keyboard he took his hands away and he managed to resist touching it again for a split-second but soon he succumbed as you can see." The guard was beaming.

It was apparent that the corpse in the chair had died from malnutrition, although the dehydration would have helped speed him on his way. To make a point, the jailer had put bottles of water and various snacks around the cell within easy reach of the prisoner. The prisoner had never attempted to even touch them..

Captain Brand allowed herself a brief smile as she walked down the plain grey corridor to her office to get to work on the next job The Dictator had given her.

Garcia's Mission

Garcia was naked except for a blindfold and tied to the bed. His body showed the tracks of recent encounters with Neeta's fingernails, or possibly Petra's. The twins did not talk much when they were torturing him. They were too busy and happy in their work.

He reflected, not for the first or last time, that some men would pay a lot of money for the treatment he was receiving for free. He smiled.

"What are you grinning about, Garcia?" It was the unmistakeable voice of Petra.

Silence would provoke pain. He remained silent by choice and was rewarded with a kiss. The kiss was provided by Petra's favourite riding whip.

"Never mind about my smile, Petra. I am always happy with you. Tell me what Captain Brand wanted."

"What about Captain Brand?"

"Well she was here. I would know her voice anywhere and the fear that comes into your tone when you talk to her."

"You hear too much. I think a knitting needle in each ear would cure you of that."

"Pardon?"

"I said I think a knitting needle in each ear would cure you of that."

"I didn't quite catch you."

A vicious punch to the solar plexus told Garcia that she had finally realised he was joking. She was perhaps thinking that making him into such a pain addict was only making him a cheeky prisoner now. That didn't stop her following up the punch with a few more and burning his nipple with a lighted cigarette. Then she saw how excited he was getting and she started getting excited too and one thing led to another. It was a good half-hour before the latest instructions from Captain Brand came back into the conversation. By now both the twins were present.

"You have another job. We are not to tell you what it is."

"That might make it a bit diffi..gh" A punch to the mouth momentarily shut up Garcia.

"We are not **supposed** to tell you what it is," continued Neeta, "but we are going to. You are to assassinate Miranda. Oh hello. Has the cat got your tongue? Were you about to tell us it is not possible?" She laughed.

"Garcia, you are among the few people who know there is more than one Miranda. Other people outside the inner circle may suspect though most people are as thick as horseshit. I can assure you that it is possible to kill a Miranda. Captain Brand made us..."

Petra corrected, "Captain Brand allowed us to watch when she killed one herself. The Miranda had displeased The Dictator in bed so that sealed the manner of her execution.

Brand lined up a dozen Romeos to use her like a piece of meat until she was dead. It was (she groped for the right word. She was weighing revulsion, excitement and the feeling of being privy to big secrets). It was instructive. Yes, instructive will do."

"Surely," Garcia objected, "the Mirandas are guarded as well as The Dictator himself is guarded. It would not be possible for a rebel assassin like myself to get that close."

"You will get close enough to kill Miranda. You will get close enough in a very public forum. I can promise you that. Some of us have unique access to Da... The Dictator." Petra offered.

"Da dictator? Da da dictator?" mimicked Garcia, "you have a stammer? You two certainly do say "dad" when you should say 'The Dictator' quite a lot don't you?"

"Neeta, get the bloody knitting needle."

"Yes. Yes. Only do one ear though. He will need to listen to his instructions and learn them."

The twins set about instructing Garcia. They took it in turns. The instruction went on all night. By dawn he was word-perfect in his instructions and he was covered from head to foot in love-bites, cigarette burns and perspiration.

He was then taken by two men to a firing range where Captain Brand herself put him through his paces with the latest automatic weapons. The people might live in poverty. Actually the people did live in poverty as Garcia had every reason to remember. Yet when it came to weapons, the

Dictatorship was up to the minute.

Captain Brand was a harsh mistress. After all she liked to boast that she had taught the twins everything they knew. Time after time a prone Garcia heard the words "Second best is not good enough." and got a kick in the exact same spot in his side. Each time it was calculated to be a little more painful.

As one hour followed another in the airless dusty firing range, his accuracy gradually improved but there was to be neither rest nor food until his scores were perfect or "just about passable" as Captain Brand put it.

"Now you will need some special training." she said. She said this with a smile which Garcia did not like the look of one little bit.

Lucy's Story

"Sister Lam, you must know that names are a big thing in The Dictatorship. You don't give your name to someone because if they have your name they can put like a spell on you or something. They can christen a wax doll with your name and then put it in the fire and when they do that you start to melt. Something like that?"

"Well I don't think that's true." Sister Lam was massaging Lucy's tired feet. It is a brilliant way to get a receptive audience.

"Well of course no. I don't believe any of that old rubbish. It is just superstition and anyway I can protect myself against it with my St Miranda amulet."

She showed Sister Lam her amulet. The Sisters of St Miranda had started producing them on an industrial scale to raise funds. They were making a big push to reach the poor and to secretly pass on their non-slogan "The Dictator will die." Sister Lam had seen for herself how poor people responded to the unexpected charity but more than that how their eyes briefly lit up when they heard the non-slogan and garbled accounts of Miranda's vision – she was now openly called Saint Miranda. After all she had had a vision hadn't she?

People talked in vague terms about The Mirror of Eternity but not as Xavier's "box of tricks" as Miranda had called it. They were talking about a mystical place of visions where Saints like Miranda could see things which were hidden to normal human eyes. Thousands of stories of The Mirror of Eternity were circulating in The Dictatorship. Some were eerily close to the truth Sister Lam and her companions had seen in Miranda's mind.

"Anyway if you trust someone with your name, then you are trusting them not to bewitch you or make you do things because they can control you with the dark arts. Well I will let you into a secret. My name really is Lucy and Delia. Both. I have a middle name. My mother always said we were too poor to afford such petit-bourgeois affectations. I think she may have been joking. Anyway I got her name, Lucy and the name of my aunt, Delia. It is funny to hear punters calling me Delia because I am prepared to bet she has never been in the back of a taxi with a man's hand up her knickers for money. She really does not look the type."

"Your aunt is still alive?" Sister Lam sometimes asked the obvious question to move the discussion along. It was amazing what confidences people will share if you massage the soles of their feet and ask them flaming obvious questions. (She had a momentary feeling of St Katherine tutting when she used the word 'flaming' even just to herself in her own mind.)

"That's what I'm saying. She is alive. She is a sister of St Miranda. She helps the poor, not round here though. Yesterday I found her new address. I got a text from Maria, you know Jenny – I don't know her real name you see.

"Maria is being very cagey about where she is but she seems to be having fun

"Text text text all day and night

And not a stinky punter in sight.

I'm a poet and didn't know it!"

It was good to see Lucy laugh. Sister Lam took the address and promised to visit Delia that very night.

Delia lived in a house in the suburbs. When Sister Lam rang the bell she steeled herself for a rough reception. She hadn't realised exactly how rough.

There are not many dogs in the poor areas of the city – the

poorest citizens regard dogs as competitors for scarce resources. So the thing that came bounding out of Delia's front door and launched itself at Sister Lam came as a complete surprise. It was the surprise rather than the dog which bowled her over.

She found herself on her back with a large muzzle in her face and a lot of dribble cascading over her as if the dog were getting ready to make a meal of her face. If you are interested, Sister Lam will tell you it is impossible to read the mind of a dog; it is too different from a human mind.

Delia stood languidly in the doorway. She was wearing a pink fluffy dressing gown although it was 2 in the afternoon. She had perfected the skill of keeping a cigarette attached to her lower lip at all times and she was practising it now. It is usual for a dog owner to make some kind of apology in these circumstances. Delia's apology took the form of shouting "What the fuck are you doing here?"

There is nothing to fear in the dreamscape, nothing can hurt you. In fact the only thing to fear is fear itself as Franklin D Roosevelt said in another context. In his case however it was just the entire world economy collapsing which was not to be feared. For Sister Lam it was a fear of the canine stretching back to early childhood and an unfortunate encounter between a toddling Tilly and an aggressive Alsatian (you may call it a German Shepherd but that is less alliterative).

Sister Lam had the strength to push the dog off – it was a

Labrador and probably more intent on making a new friend than on eating her face. She had the strength to pick it up and juggle with it although such behaviour is not advised. For the moment however she just had the ability to lie back and think of England while the Labrador started to lick her face. She assumed this was preparatory to biting chunks off of it. She could think of nothing else.

Seeing she was going to get nowhere with a silent nun under her dog, Della called the dog to heel.

"Prince. Prince." There was no response

"Come here you mangy cur." It didn't look as if her prince was going to come so she grabbed him by the collar and hauled Prince, who was protesting at being separated from his new friend, away from Sister Lam who stood up shakily and had a go at recovering her composure.

There is an old saying you are probably familiar with: "When you're up to your ass in crocodiles it is hard to remember your original objective was to drain the swamp."

"When you have a large Labrador on your face and you are more scared of dogs than you are of Wolfie, it is hard to remember which day of the week it is, never mind why you came here." is Sister Lam's version of that saying.

"Well?" demanded Delia.

"I'm scared of dogs." was all Sister Lam eventually came up with. It turned out to be a good thing to say.

"Well then you are stupid. Old Prince here is harmless. The

worst he could possibly do is to gum you to death. Look. You'd better come in and wash your face. I can't have you lying out there. Are you collecting money because I haven't got any."

"No I am not collecting money but I would like to wash my face."

When Sister Lam had scrubbed all the dog-spit and a fair amount of the epidermis off her face she sat down to talk to Delia.

"I was bitten by an Alsatian when I was a child." She began.

"That is terribly interesting," Delia said, looking pointedly at her watch, "Did you come to discuss dogs?"

"I came to discuss Lucy."

"Well you're a bit late, she died six years ago."

"Her daughter calls herself Lucy."

"Well she would it's her name isn't it. But that Lucy is nothing to do with me now."

As Sister Lam brought her own fear under control she saw two kinds of fear in Delia's mind. There was a fear that her comfortable life was going to be disrupted if she got involved in any way with her niece and over and above that there was an overwhelming fear of Lucy's pimp, "The Man." Delia saw herself being beaten and intimidated by him.

"Do you know 'The Man"?"

Delia essayed a laugh, "Do you mean Cedric?"

"Cedric."

"His father, God rot his socks, hated the little tyke from birth so he called him Cedric so that all the other kids in the street would tease and bully him. It worked too. That's why he calls himself 'The Man' now."

Sister Lam caught the thought directly from Delia's mind, Cedric was Delia's son? He is the reason she lives very nicely here in the suburbs on the money he makes from girls like Lucy? That's not quite the same as not having anything to do with her.

Out loud she said, "Do you think he beats women? Girls?"

Delia lit another cigarette before replying. She gave a reply The Man would have approved. "Only if they're out of line. He gives them a slap now and then, for their own good."

"Lucy would like to meet you. I don't think she wants anything, money or even much of your time but she thinks you are her only link with the past. Well that is, unless The Man is her cousin." Sister Lam added mischievously.

Delia sat down quickly at imminent peril to the impressive long ash on her cigarette.

"It's true what they say about you. You are in league with the Devil. How else could you know that?" She shouted.

She was breathing heavily and looking around the room as if seeking a means of escape.

Sister Lam was quite calm now. Memories of what she thought of as a dog attack were fading as fast as she could make them go. She sat and waited.

A slightly calmer Delia protested, "Look she can't come here. How can she come here. I have respectable neighbours. They hate the street girls. They think they are the lowest of the low. I would never live it down if one turned up here.

Sister Lam gave the address of the cafe. If anything Delia was more outraged. "You think I, a respectable woman with a position in The Dictatorship, would lower herself to go to that street? I will have you know I have an important job in the office of the under-secretary's assistant. It is in The Dictator's compound itself. I have security clearance to the outer circle. I cannot be seen dead or indeed alive consorting with the scum of the gutter."

Seeing the look in Sister Lam's eye she changed her tune. "Obviously I don't mean my dear niece Lucy. I mean the other girls." She shuddered convincingly.

"Well I am going to suggest we meet at St Miranda's Church. Miranda is about as respectable as you can get I would have thought."

"Not if you have heard the stories I've heard in The Dictator's compound. But you are right we could meet briefly there. You will be with us, Sister Lam?"

Sister Lam nodded

"And make sure Cedric does not know about it?"

"I promise."

Delia and Lucy

"You're sure that Cedric does not know about this?" Delia first addressed Sister Lam, scarcely acknowledging Lucy. Lucy was grinning to hear "The Man's" real name.

"It seems he is un grande fromage," Sister Lam began.

Delia frowned.

"An important person in one of the local gangs. They have a turf dispute with their rivals and they are meeting to resolve their differences tonight. He took a gun. So I think it won't be a chat over tea and cakes."

Delia smiled about that. She had no apprehension that her son might be in danger. She had just worked out what "un grande fromage" meant.

"We can talk in the Sacristy. The Sisters of Miranda will be filling the church soon."

"Those whores." Delia let out instinctively. Then she looked a little shamefacedly at Lucy and wondered if being rude about whores was the most diplomatic conversational gambit.

By way of explanation, she added, "Miranda sleeps with The Dictator every night and they believe that she can make him pay for her favours by staying his hand from oppressing the people. All I can say is, she can't be much good in bed because he hasn't let up on the common people. Not that I care about them. I work in the Dictator's Compound after all."

"Aunt Delia, it is so good to see you after all these years."

She didn't like the "Aunt" and she didn't give the impression that the feeling was mutual. She sat down to avoid Lucy's attempt to hug her. She wore a fixed smile because she didn't want to make a poor impression on Sister Lam.

She fumbled for a cigarette and was on the point of lighting it when she remembered she was in a church so it remained in her hand.

"You know what The Man, you know what Cedric makes me do, Aunt Delia?" Lucy wasn't going to be brushed aside.

"Now, Lucy. We all have to do things we don't particularly like to make a living don't we now?"

"I hate it, Aunt Delia, all those horrible old men with their smelly breath and their drunken groping in the back of the car, night after night. They're cruel and they're disgusting."

"Well of course, dear."

"I don't want to open my legs for them any more."

Lucy's directness was having an effect. At least Delia wasn't trying to ignore her. Her smile hovered between polite and genuine as if making up its mind.

"You know...Lucy... If I could I would have you come and live with me but can't you just put up with it for the time being? Until I can sort something out?"

Lucy was about to reply when the sacristy was suddenly filled, possibly for the first time, with a very loud rendition of "Smack my bitch up." Lucy grinned sheepishly and answered her phone. What she heard made her go pale.

"Well what was so important?" Delia snapped. Then she realised that Lucy was in a state of shock.

"It's" was as far as she got before she started crying. Sister Lam took her hand and she started to calm down enough to say disjointedly,

"It's...The Man."

That was enough to have Delia crying. Sister Lam could read their thoughts but said it out loud anyway, "He's been shot?"

Lucy nodded.

"Dead?"

Lucy nodded again.

Delia let out an unrestrained wail. She was weeping uncontrollably for her son and just a little bit for the comfortable life he had been able to give her. Lucy too was weeping for the man who beat her and sent her out to be abused night after night.

Sister Lam could see the effort it took for Delia to pull herself together because there was action to be taken right away.

She grabbed the phone and took out the sim card. Lucy protested. All of Delia's feelings were directed into dealing with this immediately.

"Listen, you little fool. You have to disappear. I know how this works. The gang that killed Cedric will regard you as spoils of war. They will want to run you from now on. Do you want that?"

She didn't wait for an answer.

"Well no phone calls and no texting until we are sure they have stopped looking for you. And you have to keep off the streets.

"Sister do you have anywhere she can go."

Sister Lam had plans to set up a refuge and to get Miranda to sponsor it but so far they were only plans.

"Right my girl. You are coming with me. We will light a candle for Cedric and then we're out of here. Sister Lam, you come with us."

After a look at Sister Lam she added "please" as a gesture towards politeness. Sister Lam was happy to come.

From the Diary of Xavier Hollands

When Wolfie realised that The Dictator had commissioned a documentary about his life he insisted on getting a video of it. I was concerned that he would be harder to keep on side but in the event he laughed so heartily at the video that it didn't influence him one way or another. It was apparently a mass of mistakes and even referred to Salzburg as a part of Austria at one point – that would earn his condemnation under any circumstances. His life's work was to make sure that it did not fall under the sway of Austria or Bavaria. And when the idiot translated Salzburg as "salt mountain" rather than "salt fortress" I thought he was going to wet himself in a manner of speaking.

He has even agreed that it was daft to try to keep Tilly out of The Dictatorship. Through her we now have two means of access to The Dictator, Miranda and now Delia who has access to the outer circle and presumably to the gossip of the compound. Tilly is just the person to get that information from her. Miranda's insights through The Mirror of Eternity will help us no end. They already have.

Before this is over we will have set up the Miranda safe house for the street girls. Father Alon is keen on bridging the gap between the Sisters of Miranda and the street girls. I wish him good luck with that!

So "Tilly turns up Trumps" as a schoolgirl mag of the 1950s might have put it. I am so in love with her. Here in the dreamscape we cannot make love – it would also clash with her persona as a Sister of St Katherine of course.

I imagine the reason Geert wasn't bothered when she was up to what she was up to with Kaspar (an unfortunate series of incidents I am keen to forget all about by the way) was that she didn't know, or just didn't believe the warnings. In fact it is unlikely she even believed a hard astral projection was possible until she had actually done it. That's empiricism for you.

She didn't get trapped in another reality because she was already in the reality. For her it was just a bit of safe sex on the side. And it is very very safe – physically. Psychologically I am not so sure. I don't want her to end up getting addicted to the dreamscape, for example. And what happens in dreams doesn't always stay in dreams. I still have thoughts about

Krystyna and I never met her in real life.

As for Kaspar, well he slept with (virtually at any rate) my mother and tried to kill my wife. In a Greek tragedy I would have had to kill him myself. In the event The Dictator did the job for me. And Miranda? Well she just watched him die.

Anyone who wants power has to have a touch of ruthlessness, Wolfie keeps telling me. It would seem that Miranda qualifies in that department at least. Just now the secret world of the Sisters of Miranda is buzzing with her "visions" and I have heard some of them talk (to be precise I have overheard their thoughts) about The Mirror of Eternity as if it were something Saints like her can consult to help them guide mere mortals like them. If only they knew!

Tomorrow we have another engagement with Miranda and we will see more of the "visions" she is sharing with us. The Procrastination Machine seems to be a weapon of our time. I am not sure Google and Twitter haven't already conquered the world with a Procrastination Machine of a sort. Miranda has taken to wearing gloves and she is very circumspect about opening any parcels she receives. We only see her visions "as in a glass darkly" but that does not mean they are any the less illuminating.

The Dictator

Captain Brand was standing in The Dictator's office. Here even she looked nervous. She knew that one door led to life and one to death and The Dictator alone could decide which exit she was going to take if she incurred his displeasure. And he was obviously displeased.

"These reports of the Sisters of Miranda and their secret messages. You can verify their accuracy? Verify their accuracy with your life?" He added unnecessarily.

"Dictator, I have used agents to infiltrate this organisation."

The Dictator's look said "I know that. Now get on."

"I know they are using the money from Saint Miranda talismans to reach out to the working classes as they have never done before. With the demise of Ygael the serious opposition is in disarray for now until they can find another leader. I have high hopes that Garcia – who is our man – will become that leader."

"High hopes are no bloody use, Captain. I cannot do anything with them. How do we know that Garcia won't revert to type if he becomes a leader of the opposition? And what the devil has this to do with the Sisters of Miranda?

"Garcia will remain loyal to us. We have damning evidence of his direct involvement in the killing of Ygael. If the opposition have that information we can leave his punishment to them. If that became necessary it would weaken and divide the opposition further.

"I also seek approval for a plan to use Garcia to help us solve the Miranda problem."

The Dictator nodded for Captain Brand to continue. She

suppressed a smile.

"Garcia can become leader of the opposition by masterminding a dramatic blow against the Dictatorship, the assassination of Miranda."

"From what you tell me he couldn't mastermind his way out of a paper bag. I take it that you will be the mastermind and ..." The Dictator gestured towards the red door which led to death in case Captain Brand was in any doubt of the price of failure.

"The assassination of Miranda will completely demoralise the whores. The use of the opposition to carry out the assassination will effectively prevent any alliance between the whores and the opposition. They will go back to their candles and their beads although I recommend that some should be rounded up and shot on general principle. In particular Father Alon would be better off out of this world than in it. The assassination of Miranda will provide a suitable pretext for any acts of firm government which you choose to take to secure the public safety.

"I will submit the exact details of the assassination in writing but the fundamental idea is very simple. An attempt will be made to kill off everyone at the top table at a highly public dinner. The food will be poisoned. I have lined up half a dozen security personnel who will be shot for allowing it to happen. Only you will be provided with the antidote to the poison.

"The other Mirandas will, as ever, be confined to the compound for the dinner. It will be my unfortunate duty to strangle them to maintain the public fiction that Miranda has been killed."

"It will be your duty to kill them, Captain. The hypocritical 'unfortunate' is unsuitable here and I know you well enough to know you will enjoy strangling them far more than shooting them. Don't try my patience. I have enjoyed the Mirandas and I know that they have benefited from your rigorous training. If losing them is the price I will have to pay to disarm these whores in the Sisterhood of Saint Miranda then so be it."

"I will use Neeta and Petra to assist with this task." Captain Brand continued slyly, "They have trained Garcia. He is psychologically conditioned to obey them. It would of course be an opportunity to terminate them with extreme prejudice if that option were required."

"You are to make no such plans, Captain. You are exceeding your authority in even suggesting it. And I will kill the next person who uses the phrase 'terminate with extreme prejudice' in my presence. It is ridiculous."

"Apologies, Dictator. .Shall I submit my written report – excising any suggestions of the fate of Neeta and Petra?"

The Dictator gave a gesture of dismissal. Captain Brand was thankful to exit via the green door. On this occasion anyway.

Extract from the Diary of Miranda

I shared my vision of the dictator and the odious Captain Brand with Wolfie and Xavier. It seems Sister Lam was on a mission of mercy which is typical of her – can't keep her eye on the ball. I relived my experience of seeing unseen the inner sanctum of The Dictator which I have seldom seen with my waking eyes. It has haunted my nightmares at times though. Terrible things happen there and horrific inhuman decisions are taken.

I tried to talk them through my vision but a look and a gesture from the one called Wolfie was enough to tell me that they didn't need any words. It seems they really can read minds. Is all this astral projection rubbish true? It seems more like black magic than science to me. Science and reason put paid to all superstition and religion a century ago – so The Dictator says. Although I am his bound concubine I am always to call him "Dictator" or "The Dictator". Captain Brand took great pleasure in training me in this and ruthlessly punishing any mistake I made. She did it all without leaving bruises. I now know what an electrode up the anus feels like and I think the bruises would have been preferable.

We discussed and discussed how to deal with this situation and how to turn our foreknowledge to our advantage. Wolfie had a number of ingenious schemes. He talked mainly of how we are to manage after we have turned the tables on The Dictator and he lies dead at my feet. He has a shrewd political brain almost on a par with Wolf-Dietrich himself I imagine. Machiavelli could take lessons from him rather than the other way round.

And we spent some time discussing the fate of the other Mirandas. I do not know them personally. That kind of intercourse is discouraged. There I go again, like a 19th century novelist using "intercourse" to mean discussion or interaction rather than sex. He would certainly discourage that too! Apart from Captain Brand's sadistic version, he is intolerant of lesbianism even in sex play.

As I say I do not know them personally but we cannot think of any way of saving their lives without 'revealing our foreknowledge prematurely' as Wolfie put it. I do not need the Mirror of Eternity to show me Captain Brand stripping, humiliating and strangling them one by one. 'A nice evening's work' she would call it. She would undoubtedly video it for her future amusement. I have had sight of some of her videos. They actually made me vomit.

Xavier ended the evening (it was actually 3 am; do these guys sleep? My spies tell me they don't) with an apparently irrelevant anecdote. I only realised its significance later. His exact words were,

"I attended an exam at the Institute of Education once. There were 68 of us taking one paper and one guy sitting another. The problem was the lone student had 68 papers and the rest of us just the one. It was a Sunday too so it took them an hour and a half to sort out photocopies."

I missed Sister Lam at the meeting. I shouldn't be so disparaging of her missions of mercy but they must not be allowed to get in the way. She is already talking about a safe house for the street girls like my Jenny. That is all very well and I have pledged to support it, just **not right now**.

The outer circle

Lucy settled into Delia's spare room. It was a room she used to keep for Cedric. It was a room which had never been used. The furnishings were sparse but better quality than anything Lucy was used to and there was an unheard-of en-suite bathroom. The Man was rough and ready and a bully but that didn't mean she didn't miss him like a part of herself. He had been a part of her life for years and he had been sweet to begin with but soon sweet-talked her into opening her legs for a succession of smelly old men. And when persuasion didn't work he used force. Some clients liked that, to have sex with her while The Man held her legs apart or twisted her arms, or tortured her in other ways.

She would take a long time to get used to the fact he was never coming back. Sometimes she saw a good side in him which other people could never see. The good side of him was dead now. And he would burn in Hell for what he did for her. She didn't think the gangsters allowed their victims time for a prayer of contrition.

Delia settled in the living room sitting opposite Sister Lam. She had soon acquired the inevitable bottle of firewater and her cigarette was hanging from her lower lip.

They talked in low voices to avoid waking Lucy. At first she talked about Cedric. He was a little devil as a child but death had transformed him into an angel in her mind. Sister Lam listened patiently and never let on that she realised every word was a lie and actually Delia was missing the income that came from Cedric and indirectly from girls like Lucy. Sister Lam seldom spent her wages and she had some money from the Sisters of Miranda. She was able to tactfully set Delia's mind at rest.

Delia was very well-off compared with most of the people she had met in the Dictatorship and she had a good job in the outer circle of The Dictator's compound but the drop in income would still hit her sense of security hard.

In time she got around to talking about The Dictator's compound gossip.

The outer circle was completely separate from the inner circle. Nobody could get from one to the other without going through one of two checkpoints. Except of course those who knew of another way, which was most of the staff. The cleaners invariably left a door open between the two compounds between the hours of one and two. In the unlikely event that someone wanted to go from one to the other, there it was. Getting into the outer circle was as she put it "a piece of piss." She told the guards she had lost her pass and after a lot of to-ing-and fro-ing she got another one. Then she found the old one down the back of the sofa. She left the two passes on the table.

"You know I heard a funny thing. It was about a Sister like you which is what brings it to mind. She was being held by a nasty piece of work called Quin. Now the talk was that he used to get up to all sorts of dirty business with the female prisoners if you know what I mean. Well the story went around that the filthy little tyke was about to you-know have his leg over with this sister when Saint Miranda appeared and the Sister disappeared. Astonishing. Well of course I took it with a pinch of salt. I take all the Miranda stories with a pinch of salt but plenty of folk believe them. That is to say mainly women but some men too in the army and the secret service so I am told. What I do know is that Quin certainly disappeared.

"Some say that he was a follower of Miranda and the devil took him straight off to Hell for trying to rape a Sister. He certainly went straight to Hell but I am tempted to think it was for letting a prisoner escape. Nobody gets away with that sort of incompetence.

"What they say in The Dictator's compound is that you never make the same mistake once. One mistake and you're pushing up daisies if you know what I mean. Or they hand you over to some lowlife like Quin so you end up wishing you were pushing up daisies."

Hearing her own story retold in this manner amused Sister Lam but she was careful not to show it. She wanted to hear more.

"I don't believe the Miranda stories." Delia said later when the firewater had begun to make her conversation repetitive but revealing.

"I will let you into a secret. That Miranda that you see all the time on the TV? You must have seen her, right?"

"Yes I have."

"Well I am here to tell you, strictly between ourselves, it is not always the same woman. What do you think about that?"

Delia's questions seldom required an answer and this was no exception.

"No. No. But I'm telling you, you see. Yes I know for a fact. It is a fact, a cast-iron fact. Why are facts cast iron? I don't know. It is a copper-bottomed fact that there are in actuafatality sish of them. You know, sish."

She held up six fingers, rather unsteadily.

"It's a fact. A cast-bottomed, copper-assed fact is what it is. And that Captain Brand. A Nazi piece of work. Nasty, well Nazi too" Delia had an unexpectedly schoolgirlish giggle. "Well that little Nazi has a room where she trains them in all kinds of disgusting whassits. A bedroom if you see what I..."

And she fell asleep on the table.

Sister Lam got her a cushion and wondered if her companions had got any more interesting information from their session with Miranda. Still access to the outer circle might be useful, very useful indeed. She picked up the spare pass that was just lying there.

The Banquet

It was a glittering occasion. Crystal chandeliers illuminated the great hall and the light was reflected back by the cutlery and the napery and of course the jewels brought out specially for the occasion. On the TV the announcers were gushing mindlessly about the dresses. Miranda's certainly was a work of art. It was a creation in orange and black with just enough décolleté to get the commentators overexcited. It was an article of faith that Miranda's dress had to outshine that of any other woman, just as The Dictator's after-dinner speech had to be the most wise and wonderful thing they had ever heard. The fact that the same speech was recycled in different words was not something a journalist who wanted to remain a journalist, or alive for that matter, was likely to mention or even think about.

The Dictator had drunk a phial of rather unpleasant liquid in his office before setting out. He stepped through the door and realised at once that he had stepped through the wrong door. Although the wisest individual in existence, he was completely colour-blind. The antiseptic tiling in the corridor was plain enough however and he was soon able to correct his mistake. A lesser man would have been at a loss to understand how he had managed to make such a mistake. He was never at a loss. A lesser man might have seen it as an omen but he defied augury on a daily basis.

He greeted the important guests formally and politely but unsmilingly. He was a man with the whole weight of the country on his shoulders and it was his policy not to smile in public. It was rumoured that he would only smile, and fleetingly at that, when greeting someone he was about to have assassinated. His guests were only too glad of a greeting without a vestige of a smile.

Captain Brand was there of course, keeping a close eye on events though still secretly excited about the nice evening's work she had already had with the five other Mirandas. She had been tempted to keep one or two for later but duty was duty.

Traditionally The Dictator and Miranda remained seated during the loyal toasts. The men toasted The Dictator, The women toasted Miranda. It would be the last time that event was to take place.

Captain Brand was ready to shut the doors and shut down the cameras to create the right atmosphere of emergency when Miranda and the important guests fell to the ground. The important guests would receive urgent medical attention and one or two would survive along with The Dictator. Nobody would comment in the media that they were the teetotallers in the party. Nobody in the media who wanted to be alive next week would comment anyway.

The guests were provided with a local full-bodied red wine which easily concealed the poison. Those who preferred white knew better than to quibble with The Dictator. The important guests were expendable, collateral damage to use another phrase The Dictator found ridiculously coy.

Captain Brand was unaware that some of her staff were also waiting for an event. This included the two who were stationed closest to her.

All eyes were on The Dictator as he suddenly pitched head-forward into his bouillabaisse. Instead of falling dead, Miranda and the honoured guests were on their feet in consternation. Captain Brand was seized by both arms and she felt a hypodermic in her neck. She was unable to witness how her panic drill was carried out to perfection.

The Dictator was dead. Long Live Miranda.

Previously

Garcia was understandably nervous but he had been so successfully programmed by the twins that there was no chance that he would fail in his task. The prospect of leading the Revolutionary Committee – even as a traitor – was an ambition beyond his dreams. I mean not his wildest dreams of course. His wildest dreams concerned Neeta and Petra and should perhaps be saved for another day.

He was very surprised to be intercepted by a civil servant in the Outer Circle of The Dictator's compound and ushered insistently into a side room. He was more than surprised to find Miranda and Sister Lam in the small office. For the man charged with assassinating one of them he thought he kept his cool remarkably well.

Sister Lam could almost hear his heartbeat and the turmoil in his mind was all-but-unreadable.

"Thank you, Delia." Miranda smiled at the civil servant who seemed very conscious of the honour and practically tongue-tied.

"We have all of Captain Brand's evidence about the assassination of Ygael." was Miranda's first bombshell for Garcia.

"You have met Sister Lam here. She is a truth-teller. She can tell whether you are going to do as I say or not. Be careful. Your very life may depend on it."

"What are you here for?"

"To see Captain Brand." was his eventual response.

Sister Lam nodded.

"Oh and you are going to talk about the weather? Or about your activities with Neeta and Petra? Or about assassinating me?" was her second bombshell.

"Yes."

"Which?"

Garcia looked long and hard at Sister Lam. He had met her just the once but realised she had extraordinary powers. He mentally crossed himself.

"About...about the third option."

"And if you don't Brand will tell all about you killing Ygael and if you do then of course we will. A bit of a cleft stick."

Garcia looked confused.

"A bit of a no-win situation wouldn't you say?"

They let Garcia think about that

"If this goes right, by the end of this day, I will be alive, Captain Brand will be dead and you will be well positioned to take over as leader of the Revolutionary Committee. How does that sound?

"All you need to do is this. Everyone on the top table is to have dark red wine laced with the poison?"

Garcia just nodded.

Miranda produced a small phial and a half litre bottle

"They will get dark red wine laced with this. It is harmless. The phial contains the poison. The colours match. You just have to switch. It will not be easy but you can do it. Well put it this way, you could do it if your life depended on it. It does.

"I thought Captain Brand was a tough cookie."

"That is more like the old Garcia." was Sister Lam's contribution.

She took Garcia's face between her palms and made him look into her eyes. "Repeat the instructions." Sister Lam knew this hocus-pocus was quite unnecessary but she did it anyway.

Garcia did as he was told.

"He intends to do this" she concluded, "as if his life depended on it." she added unnecessarily. In that statement was the full force of her unquenched desire to see Garcia suffer and it was not lost on him.

Revolution
"One more day to revolution,
We will nip it in the bud."

"Xavier what are you singing? More to the point why are you singing? We have serious work to do here." Wolfie sounded tetchy, even by his standards.

"It comes from *Les Miserables* which is, inter alia, a musical about a failed revolution. And that is exactly what we could have here is we neglect the ABCs."

"Yes but don't the revolutionaries all go to heaven in the last scene." Sister Lam had vague memories of the film Xavier had dragged her along to when they were courting.

"Yes but I think we need to do something in the here and now, don't you? I believe in life before death too you know. And by something I mean securing the co-operation of the military and the media. The two M's in the ABC."

"Well, Sister Lam, I know that you have what you insist on calling 'issues' with Garcia but he has actually confessed now and his sins are between him and God. For the moment, he has contacted the Revolutionary Party – who are antagonistic to the Revolutionary Committee – about a pact. They have support with the working classes and these trade unions, whatever they are exactly." Wolfie knew perfectly well what trade unions were but was just showing indifference.

"But no tanks?" Xavier's tone was all innocence.

"Stop being facetious, it ill-becomes you. Miranda tells us she has got supporters among the rank and file at least in the army. Although her support is mainly female, those young soldiers have all got mothers and sweethearts. The slogan on the streets is "The Dictator is Dead. Long Live Miranda!" and the soldiers will hear that and think twice about opening fire. They have been brought up to obey The Dictator without question but also to worship Miranda as if she were, well, a Saint." Wolfie was agnostic about whether Miranda was a Saint.

"You mean they would bayonet striking miners without a second thought but they will hesitate to act against Miranda? Well it sounds like a plan. However, we need to get the media on side or at least neutral." Xavier explained.

"The media are never neutral," Sister Lam added, "They serve the rich and powerful. We could do with the Dictator's under-secretary for communications here now couldn't we?"

"You mean?"

"Delia's boss. Miranda is bringing him here now. Her secret service people have secured the perimeter. They are double-checking ID cards since I passed on Delia's piece of information. I imagine the under-secretary will be overawed by Miranda's patronage. He is to be called 'Mr Under-Secretary' by the way. No names where possible is the rule here. Employees are often called by their payroll numbers."

Suddenly Wolfie laughed. "You know what I'm going to say." They could see in his mind a most unArchbishoplike amusement that they were using the weapons of autocracy against it. The Dictator's security services had been subverted by Miranda's supporters who had assassinated Captain Brand without a qualm. The ends justifying the means of course. "And all in the name of this Democracy of yours, Sister Lam. Wasn't The Dictator elected?"

"Well the last election was twenty years ago," Xavier pointed out, "And there was only one candidate. The old 'vote for us or we'll shoot you.' ticket."

"And you think Miranda will be better?"

"Well she has good intentions towards the poor. I can read that in her mind, as can you."

"Yes I am sure it will begin like that." was Wolfie's smug response.

The conversation was suspended when Delia (or Payroll Number 40D/487 as she was called) ushered the Under-Secretary and Miranda into the room. Miranda looked tired. Unlike the others she required sleep. The under-secretary "looked like a grey man in a suit" in Sister Lam's somewhat dismissive phrase.

Almost before they had sat down, the under-secretary started talking nineteen to the dozen, "You must address the nation and in particular a message must go out to the army. What you must tell the army is..."

"You forget who you are addressing, under-secretary. What I will say to the army is this. 'In nomine patris et filiis et spiritus sanctus," (Wolfie actually smiled at this. She had said it in Latin to please him. In the actual broadcast she translated it into the vernacular, "In the name of the father, son and holy ghost.")

"You must not mix religion and politics," the under-secretary was speaking as The Dictator had dictated to him for ten years. The Prince-Archbishop Wolf-Dietrich Von Raitenau made a noise somewhere between a snort and a laugh. It seemed particularly wolfish.

Miranda gave the under-secretary a look which said to anyone without a trace of mind-reading power "Interrupt me once more and face the consequences." The under-secretary subsided and started taking notes on his clipboard instead.

Miranda continued, without notes, "If you are given an order to strike a citizen, I will be there to stay your hand. From this day forward any order to attack the poor, any order to fire on the poor is illegal and you are not required to obey it. I am a servant of the people. You are sons of the people. You are to protect and defend them to the best of your ability. You have full licence to take action against those who order you to attack the poor.

"There are to be elections in one month from now. I will be standing in those elections but there will be other candidates. For example, my son, the young Dictator will be standing too. He is only ten years old and obviously the national assembly will have to choose an appropriate guardian for him."

The mind-readers in the room could see that she expected to get that job. The under-secretary had a shrewd suspicion. The National Assembly only met once a year to confirm The

Dictator in his post and eat a slap-up dinner. This would be a new job for them.

Now I will need to send a message to the army alone. I will deliver it in person to the garrison in the Capital but it will be televised solely for the forces channel. Is that understood? It will go out tomorrow after my first broadcast has gone out. I want announcements that there will be a special broadcast at 6 pm throughout the day. I will make the recording here in the compound.

The under-secretary was writing furiously.

"Now about you."

The under-secretary was used to that tone. Any personal address presaged very bad, possibly terminally bad, news.

"Yes, Miranda."

"I have a name. Everybody addresses me by that name. It is a personal bond between myself and the people. You are going to be my under-secretary of communications. I am buggered if I am going to call you under-secretary from here on in. I know you leave your name at the gates of the compound but without going to have a look see if you can remember it."

"Dagys, Miranda."

Miranda waited

"Darijus Dagys, Miranda." He even essayed a smile.

"Thank you, Darijus, we will be working closely together for the next period and I am entrusting you with very important work. Get Delia (and stop calling her 40D/487) to find out about a safe house in the capital. It is for the street girls, liaise with Sister Lam and mind you treat her with respect.

The Battle for the Streets

"If you wish to defeat fascism, first win the battle of the streets." said Xavier

"Who said that?" asked Miranda as he accompanied her to the barracks in a chauffeur-driven limousine.

"I did and also Leon Trotsky come to think of it. I think he said it first."

"The police (what is left of them) and the gangsters are hopelessly intertwined and rather unfortunately they are also exceptionally well-armed. I do not think we are going to win back the streets with sweetness and light, do you?"

"Sweetness, light, Kalashnikovs and tanks perhaps. You could announce an amnesty for any former gangster who comes over to the revolution. It ought to be strictly time limited though. They must come over in the next week or be shot like rabbits."

"That is your Leon Trotsky again isn't it?"

"Well he knew more about this sort of thing than I do."

"One thing is for sure. There is going to be blood on the streets. That safe house, or safe houses for the street girls are a matter of urgency."

"Well you can rely on Sister Lam to get that organised.

"Intelligence, Xavier, we are going to need intelligence. The main function of the security service is to protect The Dictatorship not to keep tabs on the gangsters. Any gangsters who come over would be useful."

"I am going to a party tonight."

Miranda was getting used to Xavier's apparently irrelevant remarks and just waited.

"The local Revolutionary Party. I am going with Garcia to try to get some kind of pact together. They will have chapter and verse on the gangsters and they do have the confidence of the poor who will inform to them if they won't inform to us.

"Changing the subject, what are the chances the local garrison will come over to you?"

"Well there is one thing you don't know Mr Clever Dick..."

"The Sisters of Miranda have sold Miranda amulets to all the rank and file soldiers." Xavier completed the thought for her.

Miranda made the sign of the cross. "You read that straight from my mind, you bastard. Look, can we have you burnt at the stake when all this is over?"

"Or possibly killed with an icepick. revolutions devour their own children. I promise you that Wolfie, Sister Lam and I will be out of here when this is over, have no fear. We will take the Mirror of Eternity with us as you requested. Our only concern will be to support the Miranda safe houses for the street girls.

You have my word. There is no need for a witch-hunt."

Miranda was smiling by the time they reached the barracks. She was surprised to be greeted by the sergeant on the gate.

"Long live Miranda!" was apparently the watchword of the day.

"Where is the commanding officer?"

"The CO is now confined to quarters with about half of the other commissioned officers. They ordered us to fire on the poor. We arrested them. It was a (he thought for a moment) historical offence."

"You mean they didn't do it after my edict of yesterday?" Miranda demanded.

"Revolutions use retrospective legislation to legitimise themselves. The American revolution just as much as the Russian." Xavier said approvingly.

"They are only confined to quarters awaiting your decision, Miranda." With the last word the sergeant seemed to realise what an extraordinary moment this was.

A wrong decision would cost him his life. The fate of the revolution, not for the first or last time, hung in the balance. Would Miranda approve the shooting of the officers? It was the only safe thing to do. Imprisonment means nothing in a civil war. The officers could be liberated by other reactionaries at any time. If the officers were reinstated those who imprisoned them would be for the high jump.

The rank and file were assembled in the courtyard. There

was a dais from which they wanted Miranda to address them. She only had the time that it took to walk from the main gate to the dais to think out what she was going to say. Her step did not falter and the sergeant fell into step beside her.

"Hail Miranda!" the troops shouted loyally and then fell silent to hear what she had to say.

They were all wearing St Miranda medallions as if it were part of their uniform. If they were apprehensive about the outcome they didn't show it.

"I have made a decree that it is no longer lawful to strike the people or to fire on the poor. I know that you have obeyed orders to do so in the past. That is forgiven. For those who issued the orders it is another matter. Bring them out in handcuffs." The last was an aside to the Sergeant who seemed to be the closest to being in charge of anyone there. He gave the job to two subordinates.

"From today you will be defending the people not attacking them. In time you will earn their trust and side by side drive the scum off the streets."

The other ranks cheered. They cheered even louder to see the commissioned officers in handcuffs. The visual impact of seeing the people who used to bully and order them about humiliated was the best sign that Miranda was going to be on their side.

"Sergeant?"

"177502, Miranda."

"I will ask you your name later. It is about to go into the history books."

Using the microphone, she addressed the troops again.

"Sergeant 177502 will appoint one NCO and one ordinary soldier. Together they will move rapidly to court martial these traitors. The only possible sentence, if they are proven to have ordered violence against the poor, is death. That sentence, where it is passed, will be suspended for those officers who devote themselves wholeheartedly to winning over other officers to the revolution.

"I used the words 'ordinary soldier' just now. Together we can do extraordinary things. We can make the streets safe, we can clear out the pimps and the drug dealers. Under orders some of you have been ruthless with the poor, you will make amends for that a hundredfold by being ruthless with the real enemies of the people. And know this, the only gangsters who will survive will be the ones who come over to the revolution in the next week.

"I am relying on you ordinary soldiers. I am relying on your trusted NCOs. May God bless you, the father, son and holy spirit."

The peroration was almost drowned out by applause and cries of "God bless Miranda!" which echoed round the courtyard. Miranda and Xavier left in their far-from-ordinary limousine.

"I thought that went rather well." She said modestly.

"It was years of work by the Sisters of Saint Miranda paying off, I suspect. A first class advance job. Can you trust the officers to genuinely go over to the revolution though?"

"Mmm I think so. With Sergeant 177502 to keep a watchful eye on them I imagine it is possible."

"His name is Marach and he has supported the Revolutionary Committee in the past."

"You read all of that in his mind? You really are the spawn of Satan, Xavier." Said with a smile it was almost affectionate.

"Speaking of spawn of the devil, is there any news of Neeta and Petra?"

"Not as yet."

Neeta and Petra

Neeta and Petra were nowhere to be found. They were in a situation which was not as unusual for them as you might think. They were in a windowless underground dungeon, naked and chained to the walls. The toilet facilities could be described as rudimentary and they had not been fed.

They were dozing lightly so that they did not hear as the door was quietly opened.

Garcia threw a bucket of cold water over Neeta. "Good morning, loose end. A bit of a rude awakening."

Petra was fully awake when her bucket of cold water hit home. "Good morning, loose end."

He spoke over their storm of abuse. "Well how are you two?

A bit peckish, perhaps? I've got a lovely Tikka Masala next door, you can probably smell it. I was thinking you might like a meal but you don't seem that interested."

"When are you letting us out of here, you low-life? You do know who our father is?" Neeta screamed.

"Yes he's dead."

That shut them up, as he intended.

Into the sudden silence in the echoing dungeon he said,"You hated him for all of your lives and you didn't even want me to know he was your father. But now he's dead. And now what are you? You are like me. You are like any of the ordinary people. You are nothing."

No physical pain could have reached them. They had been trained and tortured by Captain Brand. She had always called herself the best in the business and nobody had ever argued with her.

"Your lives are worth nothing. You wouldn't think twice about having common people killed. I am your only lifeline. I want you alive. I want you to suffer. I will be back with some food tomorrow. Well possibly, I am busy these days.

"Your friend Captain Brand used this room. She used it when she was training me. Among the bloodstains on the walls are some of mine. Some of them would be hers but she died instantly a split second after The Dictator, or I should say 'Daddy', died.

"He died far too quickly to my mind but then, as you are

about to find out, I am a deeply vindictive man.

"You will have lots of time here. You know I cannot let you out alive but you can spend your time working out what would perhaps persuade me to let you out alive.

"Behind that grill and that one, which unfortunately you cannot reach, are concealed cameras. She had lots of videos – perhaps for training purposes I don't know – of her torturing people, sometimes to death. Do you think she should have warned them, 'Your torture may be recorded for training purposes.' ? It would have been only fair, wouldn't it?"

The door shut softly behind him and the light was switched off. They had twenty four hours of darkness ahead of them.

"Are you sorry he's dead?" Neeta eventually asked.

Petra seemed too upset or too numbed to answer. Neeta knew she had to snap her out of it if she were to survive at all. She did not care, if she indeed knew, that Garcia's microphones would pick up every whispered word in this cell.

Every ounce of sisterly venom was in her tone as she continued, "Well of course you're crying. You are the weak one. You were always the weakling, the little milksop, the little cry-baby. Petra. Petra. Petra. Daddy's poor little darling."

Petra knew exactly what Neeta was doing. It still worked. She made a valiant effort to claw Neeta but Neeta had moved away to the furthest extent of her chain and Petra's fingernails clawed the wall instead.

"You fucking bitch." she shouted and the conversation

continued in that vein for a while. In the end they got back to talking normally.

"Did you hurt your nails? I am sorry about that. Come here, I'll kiss them better."

"So how do we solve a problem like Garcia?"

Petra responded by singing it, "How do you solve a problem like Garcia, How do you catch a cloud and pin it down?"

Neeta laughed explosively, "A fat smelly cloud then."

"a cloud of vindaloo flatulence!" Petra joined in.

"A flibbertijibbet! A will-o'-the wisp! A clown!"

They talked on and off just so as to pass the hours. They could not sleep. For the first time in their lives they knew what it was like to be kept awake by hunger. They speculated about what was happening in the world outside and whether Garcia had got the leadership of the Revolutionary Committee for killing The Dictator and whether Miranda had died too.

"Mummy!" Neeta cried out and they both collapsed in laughter. The cell microphones had probably never recorded quite so much laughter. Captain Brand only laughed to humiliate a prisoner. When she was torturing she was totally professional, as you would expect.

This was not quite the scene Garcia was hoping for but he noted the twins were looking drawn despite their hilarity. Another bucket of water each and the laughter subsided.

"Well I've got something for you." He said and produced a massive pizza box.

When they opened it, there was just paper and pens inside.

"If you ever want to eat, you will realise that you could seriously compromise me. You are going to write and then read, for the cameras, two confessions which I will dictate to you. You will take the blame for everything and in time I will release you and feed you well and find you a little job which will help you keep body and soul together, assuming you have them.

"Well of course I know you have bodies," (was that a trace of the old Garcia in his leer? Yes it was certainly there) "but souls, I don't think so."

They spat on the paper and threw the pizza box at him. He opened the door. They saw it had a single chalk line on it. Garcia smiled as he added another one and closed the door. The light went off again. They heard Garcia talking about saving electricity but they really weren't paying attention.

There came a day when he had drawn a five-barred gate on the door when Neeta and Petra agreed to the confessions. Garcia went over and over them until the girls were word-perfect. There were two security men in the outer room casually peeking at the naked girls and then looking away when they looked up. They had both been recruited by the Revolutionary Committee.

"Now for lunch!" he said brightly and went back outside. He came back with both hands behind his back, a joker to the last.

They were half-expecting the two machine-pistols in his hands. It was the only safe course for him. The sound of the firing was horrific in the confined space but they didn't get to hear it for very long. Revolutionary Committee Chairman Garcia walked from the cell

"Clear up the mess." He said over his shoulder as he left.

"Yes, Chairman." The security men complied with alacrity.

The Dictator's Funeral

It was a day of light drizzle. It was also a day of high tension for Miranda. "He was my husband. Yes I know I was one of six bound concubines but the public are not to know that. I am to play the role of a grieving widow."

"We know that Captain Brand, Neeta and Petra are the conveniently deceased suspects in the case," added Wolfie impassively. "For myself I reiterate my belief that you acted in self-defence and you could have chosen to bring all that out into the open."

"Would you have done so?"

"You are in power and you intend to remain so!" was all the answer she got from Wolfie. The two had grown, well not exactly friendly, but they did like each other at least. The others had noticed that nowadays she tended to take Wolfie's advice. And they noticed that the more Machiavellian the advice, the more likely she was to take it.

The army secured the streets to the cemetery although there was still fighting raging in other parts of the capital. The

Dictator had ordered a massive and massively ugly mausoleum. Wolfie thought that the whole edifice was thoroughly repulsive and therefore totally appropriate.

"The people know," Sister Lam spoke carefully, "that you held back the hand of The Dictator from striking the poor and defenceless and I think that you should hold on to that. Grieve as a widow but your power depends on the poor and they are not grieving. For the first time they can say what they think of The Dictator. And none of what they are saying is exactly complimentary.

"And then look forward to a brighter future. There is a little financial matter which may help." Xavier had been examining The Dictator computer system. He described the security as "child's play" but he had been up all night with this child's play.

"It is the little financial matter of seven billion dollars in a numbered Swiss bank account to which we – or to be exact you – now have access. It seems to me that The Dictator left this money hidden away precisely so that his passing could be marked with gifts to the people. I expect he wanted to endow hospitals and schools, which would of course be dedicated to Saint Miranda. I am sure that is what he would have wanted."

"And a Miranda bonus to the gallant soldiers who are winning the battle of the streets, perhaps." Chipped in Wolfie with his characteristic smile.

Miranda's expression broke into a grin of genuine pleasure which she had to quickly suppress because it was time for the funeral procession to move off. The gun-carriage bearing the coffin followed by the black limousines drove out of The Dictator's compound into the silent streets lined with armed soldiers.

The young Dictator, who had wisely decided against a political career, read *Crossing the Bar* by Tennyson. Appropriately enough it includes the line "may there be no sadness of farewell,"

Miranda looked suitably subdued. She talked about death and parting. She talked about God's forgiveness. Many in the poor quarters watching on TV afterwards commented, 'It is just as well God is going to forgive him because I'll be damned if I will."

The "looking forward" section of the speech got the most attention. They didn't necessarily believe that things were going to get better under Miranda but it was such a long time since anyone had talked to them of hope that they wanted to believe. The Miranda bonus which she announced went to all public servants, not just the Army so suddenly there was more money around to give the anticipation of hope some concrete form.

For the first time, Miranda introduced a minimum wage. People were very cynical of that. The gangsters did not obey any law so a minimum wage would be just another law to ignore.

The House Miranda built

If the prospect of a nun giving them operational instructions seemed odd to the soldiers of Miranda they did not show it.

"You will need to go in civilian dress. People will think you are soldiers but they won't be sure. We can use the uncertainty. If anyone asks who you are, you just say you are "revolutionaries." without revealing any more than that if possible.

"You will take sub-machine guns (the 2LRs) but try to keep them under wraps for as long as possible. Everyone will be carrying side-arms (except me obviously)" (At last a smile)

"All you are doing is picking up street girls. I don't want to know if you have done that before so don't tell me. Keep physically apart from each other but try to keep the other members of the squad in view.

"The cars will have no military markings but all of them have "MI" number-plates. The street patrols will know who you are.

"Everybody will be issued with a mobile phone. Do not use your own phone. Use the one you are given."

"The girls are to be persuaded not forced and they will be taken to the safe houses. Any questions?"

To the soldiers "Any questions?" was a formality. They were never expected to question orders from The Dictator. Old habits die hard.

"One final thing then. If any of you have sex with any of these girls Miranda will have your testicles on toast for breakfast. I think she prefers eggs."

It was a relief to be able to laugh because this was not going to be a laughing party. The gangsters would soon get wind of what was happening and Miranda had already drawn up plans to repel a full-scale assault on the safe houses.

A lot of the cars which kerb-crawled had tinted windows so Sister Lam had no problem concealing her presence while her companion asked the inevitable, "How much darling?"

His 'darling' looked him up and down and named a fee. His incognito was helped by the fact that The Dictator's soldiers did not pay. They only took. There was no law to stop them and even countries which have laws don't have laws to protect street girls from being robbed by clients.

An uncle lurked in the shadows. The girl got in ready to shed the few clothes she was wearing straight away but she was pulled up sharply when she saw Sister Lam.

"Sister Lam what the fuck...I mean what and how. What is going on here? Am I not going to get my money? My uncle will kill me."

"The uncle is not going to be killing anybody." It was the soldier who spoke.

The girl was scared. Sister Lam tried to stay calm to calm her. "There is going to be trouble tonight. It is not going to be safe on the streets."

"It's never safe on the streets."

"There will be a shoot-out between the revolution and the gangsters on this street tonight. Miranda has stayed the hand of The Dictator for good. Any uncles who do not come over and do not come over immediately will not see the dawn."

"I can see you are frightened but we are going to take you to a safe place. I am with the soldiers because you know that you can trust me. You must come and you must come freely."

Sister Lam could see the soldier was disappointed that the girl was shying away from him now he wasn't a client.

"How old is your sister, Michael?"

Without asking how Sister Lam knew his name and the fact he had a sister, he replied. "Well she is only fifteen."

"And you're fourteen aren't you, Sarah?"

"I'm twelve."

"I know that is what you tell the clients, Sarah. We are not clients. Michael has a sister of a similar age. He wouldn't want her to do this job. That is why he is going to help me get you to a safe house away from the fighting. Will you come?"

Sarah nodded and the taxi sped away. She did not see her uncle Marcos go down in a hail of bullets later that night. There really was blood on the streets that night.

Sister Lam had waited to see Sarah settled before heading out again. Sarah wanted to come with her to help other girls. She wanted her friends to be safe.

Sister Lam worked all through the night. She was saving the lives of pimps as well as street-girls. The army still had a "shoot first and ask questions afterwards" attitude which was hardly surprising given their training. Sister Lam had ways of disarming gangsters not available to the army and she was completely fearless.

She later told Xavier that she felt Doctor Katherine watching over her during that long night.

Some of the Sisters of St Miranda still thought themselves superior to the street girls and they tried to lord it over them. Sister Lam would have none of it.

"You are to treat them like your own children. It is what Saint Miranda wants you to do." They were slightly in awe of Sister Lam and her uncanny knack of knowing just what they were thinking. They listened to her and obeyed even when in their heart of hearts they *knew* they were superior to the disgusting street girls.

They didn't like to think how many fathers and husbands knew these girls only too well, knew them physically at least.

One thing their revealing clothes did reveal was just how thin they all were. This got the Sisters of St Miranda happily cooking chicken soup and the girls happily eating it. At the same time they were all trying to ignore the sound of gunfire in the city, now and then it seemed nearer, as if it were in the street outside. Anxious looks through shutters told them that was false. Sometimes it seemed further away but still too close for comfort.

Sergeant Michael eventually reported back to Sister Lam after his spell on patrol. "We are winning the battle of the streets, Sir, er Sister. A hundred gangsters are dead. They will never intimidate these girls again.

"How many have come over?"

"Well there was that one you spoke to and erm...I think a couple of others.

"Intelligence, Sergeant. We want every bit of information they can give us. And we need more of them to come over.

"The Revolutionary Party..."

"Those wankers!"

"Sergeant."

"Sorry, Sir Sister." She laughed at that.

He called her 'Sir Sister' from then on. She explained that they had information from the Revolutionary Party (I don't know whether they masturbate or not) and so far it had been accurate about the disposition of the gangsters.

"Miranda wants them to come over to us. Tell them that. They know the legends of Miranda as well as you do. This is not my whim, Michael, it is Miranda's wish. Pass that fact on whenever you can."

"Yes Sir Sister." He grinned widely, saluted smartly and went about his business.

It was 3 am. Michael should have gone off shift but somehow Sister Lam had convinced him he was doing extraordinary work for Miranda and he volunteered for another turn of duty although he knew very well that he was going to be very tired when it was finished.

He wasn't doing all this to get a promotion, he told himself. This was a man who had seen his superior officers in handcuffs. That sight had put a substantial dampener on his thirst for promotion. He was doing all this out of a liking for Sister Lam, if liking was the right word. And it was because he had never done any work like this before. He had done terrible things in the service of The Dictator. On balance he had killed more children than he had saved that night. He thought of it as atonement.

He returned to Sister Lam in the company of Father Alon and another man who gave his name as Nelson. He wore a black patch over one eye but his arms and legs seemed to be in good working order, unlike his illustrious namesake.

He said he was the commander of the secret police who had infiltrated the gangs in the Capital on behalf of The Dictator. He had come to Father Alon because he wanted to offer their surrender to Miranda. He would only offer their surrender to Miranda in person.

Sister Lam could see that his name actually was Nelson but the eye patch was an affectation. Once he sat down to be interrogated, his thoughts were filled the most horrible images his mind could conjure up, and he could conjure up quite a lot. He had heard of Sister Lam and used this simple defence to prevent her reading his mind. She decided that she would have to try to shock him out of it. This explains her choice of words. She quoted Terry Pratchett.

"Buggering arseholes, Nelson. raping little girls? Little boys? Who do you think you are, Jimmy Saville."

Nelson just smiled and thought in vivid images about torturing nuns to death.

Sister Lam lunged forward and tore off his eye patch.

"A miracle, Nelson. You can see again."

This tactic gave her a split-second insight into his mind. It was enough. It told her that he wanted to see Miranda in order to kill her. Like Captain Brand, he got a sexual thrill out of strangling women.

She took his wrists and forced his hands around her throat.

"You want to strangle Miranda? Well I think that it's time for a bit of practice, Nelson."

Michael pushed the muzzle of his machine gun into Nelson's side but Sister Lam gestured to him to hold his fire.

Nelson was bemused but only too pleased to strangle Sister Lam. The grin on his face turned to dismay as he applied more and more pressure to her throat and she looked him steadily in the eye. She didn't even change colour. After a minute she brushed his strong arms aside as if she were swatting a fly. In that minute she had the full story.

Nelson really was the commander of the secret police attached to the gangs. They really were ready to surrender.

The gangsters, however, had videos of some of the horrors he had visualised and they had blackmailed him into planning this desperate attempt to kill Miranda with his bare hands.

She felt an absolute certainty that he could be turned but there was something to do first.

"Get down on your knees." she said quietly. "You failed to kill a nun, what possible chance do you think you would have against a saint?"

Nelson avoided her eyes.

"Father Alon, are you ready to take this man's confession? We will leave you in here alone."

Father Alon knew perfectly well the risk involved in being alone with Nelson but the chance of saving his soul was more important to him.

When his confession was over, and it didn't take as long as you might think, Sister Lam came back in. Father Alon looked as if he had had a hard night's work. Michael was still pointing his 2LR sub-machine gun at Nelson and his finger was on the trigger.

Nelson thought his last hour had come. He did not expect Sister Lam to offer him a deal.

"Commander, if your men come over to Miranda, we have every chance of putting the gangsters in a position where they cannot blackmail anybody. How do you rate your chances of doing that? Imagine your life depended on your answer." She hated herself for adding that threat.

Nelson suddenly saw a lifeline, a way out. He knew there could be no lying to Sister Lam. He had to say exactly what he meant.

"The risks are great and a number of my comrades will die if we double-cross the gangsters. I should be there with them. We will fight for Miranda. I don't need to tell her in person. You can do that for me. I can't read minds but I know that you will tell the truth."

"He is telling the truth. Let him go, Sergeant." Sister Lam said authoritatively.

Michael looked as if he were going to argue but there was no gainsaying Sister Lam and he knew it.

He used the opportunity while escorting the prisoner out of the safe house to explain to Nelson the dire consequences which would follow if he were to break his word.

"I will personally douse you with petrol and set you alight. You know that is no idle threat. You have worked for The Dictator too."

Nelson did not argue.

Commander Nelson

Following the tradition of The Dictator, The Boss was only ever referred to as "The Boss". People who had lost the will to live sometimes called him "Fu Manchu" although frankly he was about as Chinese as Christopher Lee. In his office there was a portrait of The Dictator, now decorated with black ribbon.

He had nocturnal habits and it was rumoured among the gangs that he practised black magic and voodoo under the cover of darkness. When The Man was eliminated the last group of street girls in the city came under his control. His driver went out and collected one of the street girls who looked youngest and then delivered them to The Boss's house on a regular basis. They did not always come back.

Nelson had taken part in acts of violence and child abuse at The Boss's house. This was a rare honour for a gang member. The Boss regularly watched the videos made on those occasions and each time he did so he was surer that Nelson would do as he was told rather than have these videos handed over to a friendly journalist.

So when Miranda's army began its determined push against the gangs and started spiriting the street girls away from under his nose, The Boss was not perturbed. Soon Miranda would be dead and the army could go back to its proper role of keeping the Revolutionary Party and the other lot under control. And as for those whores of the Sisters of Saint Miranda – he had plans for those bitches which didn't bode well for them, or for their life insurance companies.

He switched from the video to the television. It was that bloody Father Alon again. Was he ever off the TV these days? He was urging people to pray for the soldiers of Saint Miranda and for the souls of the gangsters.

"I'll be damned if I will let that sanctimonious swine pray for my soul."

His words were truer than he knew.

There was a knock at the door. He was one of those people who call out "Come." when a subordinate knocks. Of course in his mind, everybody was his subordinate.

"It's Nelson to see you, boss."

"Show him in."

Unlike The Dictator, The Boss provided seats for his visitors and usually a drink. Nelson looked as though he needed one. He drained the glass of firewater in one go, held the base and smashed it on the table. Before he knew where he was, The Boss had a faceful of broken glass to contend with and Nelson was strangling him one-handed.

The Boss desperately hit the button on his desk to summon his bodyguard. Nothing happened. He was starting to black out for the last time and missed Nelson saying, "Here let me do that for you!" and hitting the button himself.

The bodyguard were nursing slit throats and unable to attend. Nelson had wasted no time in mounting an attack on the gangsters he had protected for all his professional life. He had their names and addresses (or at least places they could be found). There would be no nonsense about surrendering. They would not survive the night.

The Boss had one trick up his sleeve. Well actually it was a knife. Nelson saw the knife out of the corner of his eye and managed to grab it with his free hand. It went straight through his hand but The Boss was losing consciousness and would soon be dead. Nelson bit back a cry of pain and focussed on finishing the job. Finishing the job entailed stabbing The Boss a number of times after he was already dead. Nelson might be working for Miranda now but he was no pussy.

He had two hours. His men knew the order of battle they had drawn up and they accepted his statement that he would be searching The Boss's computer system for evidence while they tracked down and killed the leading gangsters. Most of them realised that "searching for evidence" was a prelude to destroying it. The secret police were too closely entwined with the gangsters to publish their secrets.

He ran an external operating system on the computer to bypass any passwords and systematically destroyed the content of the hard disk and backups. The process was automatic. While it was going on, Nelson scoured the room.

Some videos were in the desk and he destroyed them. The safe was hidden behind the picture of The Dictator. The picture was dropped to the ground and Nelson stood on it. Now there was something he wouldn't have thought of while The Dictator was alive.

You don't get far in the secret service without being able to get into a safe. In this case blackmailing The Boss's secretary had given him the combination. There was always a weak link and he was adept at finding it.

He didn't think about his own weak links as he struggled to open the safe one-handed. He had been trained and tortured by Captain Brand. Pain was just pain, he took pride in his ability to overcome it. He didn't notice that the wound in his hand was pouring blood down his clothes until it was too late. He was intent on destroying the videos from the safe when he passed out.

His men found him in the morning. His body was cold. His blood mixed with that of The Boss. They wondered what to do with the videos, destroying them seemed the best course and it was what Commander Nelson would have wanted.

Three Inquisitive People

"So you want to visit Fu Manchu's lair?"

"How are the mighty fallen. Yesterday it was fatal to mock The Boss. Today it is the done thing." Wolfie always instinctively disapproved of disrespect, even disrespect of an enemy.

The streets were unnaturally quiet. Clean-up teams were quietly going about the business of cleaning the bodies and blood off the streets. Most of the people were keeping off the streets for choice. Nobody knew if the battle against the gangsters was actually over.

They saw the once-unthinkable sight of members of the Revolutionary Committee and the Revolutionary Party working together with the soldiers of Miranda.

"If she can make peace between those groups, I think there is hope that Miranda can get the country behind her." Sister Lam suggested.

"Mmm. I note that the Revolutionary Committee are running a candidate against Miranda for the election and the Revolutionary Party are backing Miranda, I have got that round the right way?"

An unusually thoughtful Xavier nodded absent-mindedly.

"And I do believe the candidate will be your old friend Garcia." Wolfie couldn't help needling Sister Lam.

"The mass-murdering turncoat you mean?"

"The same. Although I doubt if he will be putting that on the ballot paper. You know more about these spurious democratic niceties than I do."

"Spurious?" Sister Lam always rose to the bait.

"Mm This will be an election in which there is effectively only one candidate. The opposition is split and only delusions of grandeur can have persuaded Garcia to stand. The young Dictator has decided to concentrate on his studies. Miranda has been worshipped as a Saint. It is an electoral farce."

"But Wolfie, you would support Miranda?" Xavier seemed to be coming out of his reverie.

"I stand by autocracy. Miranda will be a very good autocrat. She is already planning schools and hospitals rather than guns and tanks. And the work rescuing the street girls was, well I won't use the word 'saintly' but a lot of people will be using exactly that word."

Xavier was on the verge of asking innocently whether they could assume Miranda wouldn't engage in rash military adventures against her neighbours, as a certain Prince-Archbishop had done four centuries ago. However, their conversation was interrupted as they arrived at The Boss's HQ. It was part town-house and part fortress.

Nelson's men were in command of the building and the bodies had not been moved. The three walked into the room with varying emotions. On their travels they had seen quite a few dead bodies and since their astral projections had no sense of smell, the dead were not obnoxious to their senses.

Xavier examined the computer. Nelson's external operating system on a memory stick was still there and it showed the hard drive had been comprehensively wiped. The safe was open but all the DVDs had been destroyed beyond repair. There was a lot of money which Sister Lam appropriated on the spot for the Miranda homes.

Xavier gave orders to the secret police as one to the manner born. He wanted a very detailed plan of the building with measurements. Not tomorrow. Today.

They went through the desk but The Boss had not much in the way of paperwork. The answer-phone had been wiped and any messages were beyond recovery even by the arcane arts to which Xavier resorted.

Wolfie examined the bodies. The Boss had been subjected to a frenzied attack but the lack of bleeding suggested strongly that this had taken place after his death. Death had been by strangulation. This was known to be Nelson's preferred modus operandi whether his victims were male or female.

Nelson had obviously been intent on **something** because he ignored the serious injury to his hand which seemed to be his only injury. He had ignored it to the point that he had bled to death.

However the breakthrough came through thanks to Xavier's request.

"You were quite right sir."

"Xavier."

"Well Sir Xavier you were quite right. The measurements show that there is another room to which there is no visible entrance."

The Boss didn't have anything so crass as a button or a sliding panel. He never carried a mobile phone but fiddling with his rather large watch, Xavier stumbled across the app to open the door to the secret room.

In the room were what looked like a TV, a chair with restraints and a computer which proved to be standalone, not connected to the internet or to The Boss's network.

Xavier got to work on the computer straight away.

There were a number of video files in chronological order. The earlier ones showed horrific scenes of violence against men and women, boys and girls which had clearly been captured by concealed video devices in this room.

Some of the videos showed torture used to obtain information but the torture went on and on long after the information had been extracted. Few victims survived. Others, particularly the ones involving street girls, were purely for the gratification of The Boss, Nelson and other chosen henchmen. There were also scenes involving members of The Dictator's Inner Circle. This must have been the source of material for blackmail on a massive scale.

The later ones were difficult to comprehend. In video after video, Street girls were injected with drugs, tied to the chair and then astonishingly left to watch the TV and describe what they saw. Many of them were not able to see anything. Some of them clearly died from an overdose of whatever they were being injected with.

"It looks like a bizarre experiment." Xavier remarked.

"What it looks like is an attempt to replicate The Mirror of Eternity." Wolfie said quietly.

The Mirror of Eternity

To begin with the street girls gave incoherent and rambling accounts of what they thought they could see in The Mirror of Eternity. The Boss then took a delight in disposing of them in the cruellest ways he could imagine. There were to be no witnesses.

Then in one of the later videos they watched as a child gave a horrified account of the deaths of Neeta and Petra. It confirmed everything they thought they knew about Garcia and his former handlers but it gave a lot of detail they hadn't been aware of before.

That child survived. Xavier assumed The Boss had thought it was not just the drugs that made the Mirror of Eternity effective but also the personality of the viewer. This fitted in with his own theories but he was not happy about sharing them with The Boss.

The child, she was just called "whore" by The Boss, repeated a conversation between the leaders of the Revolutionary Party and the Revolutionary Committee.

"'Death to The Dictator' is a redundant slogan now. It is a matter of what to do with the Dictatorship. This totally vindicated what we have always said."

("A bit of boasting from The Revolutionary Party," Xavier interjected. Wolfie nodded impatiently.)

" "Well I just ask you to remember that the death of the dictator would not be one of the irrelevant issues if I had not killed him. The Revolutionary Committee believes in deeds not words. And you are right, we must look forward not backwards.

"It seems that the army in the capital has been successfully subverted, not by you and not by us."

("It's the same man. The one who killed the girls." explained the child)

"Yes but it has been subverted by Miranda. Our position is that Miranda will only continue the dictatorship under another name."

"Yes. That may well be the case but soon the army of Miranda, which has a lot of popular support, will be going into action against the gangsters in the city. This is a major split in the Dictatorship's power base. The old saying has it that 'the enemy of my enemy is my friend. I am going to suggest that we assist the enemy of our enemy. We help the army of Miranda to crush the gangsters and we participate in the forthcoming election."

"I agree, or at least we will discuss, the first proposal but the

Revolutionary Party does not participate in any bourgeois electoral farce."

(There was a noise of approval for that from Wolfie and Xavier considered making a membership application to the Revolutionary Party on his behalf).

"Well I intend to use what you term the bourgeois electoral farce for publicity but also as a way to get close enough to Miranda to eliminate her as I eliminated The Dictator."

The discussion after that was an anticlimax. Garcia was planning to kill Miranda. It stunned the three listeners but it was not enough to stop the Revolutionary Party from arguing further.

The Boss obviously decided that the child who had that piece of information could not be allowed to live, even as a prisoner. It was the final video.

"I take it this is not the meeting you attended, Xavier?"

"You take it correctly, Wolfie. I would have conveyed that information to you immediately."

Wolfie just nodded. He seemed to be the one who was deep in thought now. Eventually he said, "There seems to be no evidence against Garcia which we can use. The three people who could have testified against him are dead."

"What about the thousands who saw him poisoning the congregation at St Michael's?" Sister Lam broke in.

"He killed The Dictator, Sister Lam. And consequently Miranda gave him a free pardon. His involvement in the massacre, which is still regarded as a piece of factional warfare by the general public, will dampen his chances of electoral success certainly. But haven't we just found out that he is not interested in electoral success?"

"We will have to tell Miranda."

"Yes, Sister Lam but more to the point I think, we will tell the Sisters of Saint Miranda. With that information, who knows what they might do." Wolfie seemed grimly pleased with this. He was not sure what they could do against the Revolutionary Committee or for that matter how widely their influence spread. They had been quietly preparing the ground for Miranda's accession to power for many years.

"I wonder," Xavier was off into another apparent irrelevancy, "why the Revolutionary Party is not taking part in the election. In effect, they are endorsing the candidacy of Miranda, wouldn't you say?" His friends could see his secret thoughts. He thought the Sisters of Miranda had somehow infiltrated the male-dominated Revolutionary Party.

"First thing's first. We have to tell Miranda and we have to somehow convince her of the validity of our information." Wolfie was taking charge.

Saint Miranda

"I will kill the bastard with my bare hands!" was the distinctly unsaintly response of Miranda when she heard about Garcia's plans. To her it was, after all, just the latest example in a long line of treachery.

"In which case, it wouldn't exactly be a free election." Wolfie commented drily.

Miranda thought about that. "So you think that his electoral ambitions will safeguard him. Anything which I do against him will be seen as a violation of the democratic process. The people are so new to democracy that I cannot take that risk. This election will have to be whiter than white" She sighed, "Even if it means letting that toerag get away with ..."

"Well he is not going to get away with anything is he? I suggest that you won't want to have any talks with him without also having Sister Lam or myself present, perhaps both of us. We are more effective than the average bodyguard. And Garcia knows it."

If you talk of the Devil, so it is said, then he appears. This can't be true in general but the fact of the matter is that Delia knocked on the door to announce that Garcia was respectfully seeking an audience with Miranda to discuss the arrangements for their televised debate.

"Tell him that the under-secretary for communications will deal with the matter."

"I don't know that you should do that. It might just let him know we suspect his intentions. Also the whole democratic (Wolfie was tossing up between 'farce' and 'façade' but eventually settled on 'process') process requires equal treatment for the candidates."

"Wolfie, I remind you for the last time, I am Miranda. Delia, you know what to do."

Delia virtually bowed as she left the room. She had never been in the inner circle of the compound and so close to the new centre of power.

Garcia was not pleased. He had no plans to assassinate Miranda that day but his dignity as the leadership candidate in the election had been harmed. He was angry with Miranda but very friendly, some would say over-familiar, with Delia.

"I am going to insist on equal time for both speakers." he began aggressively.

"So is Miranda," a calm and relaxed Darijus responded. "It must be fair and it must be seen to be fair. At the beginning, in front of the cameras, you will toss a coin to decide who speaks first. We have no intention of using a double-headed coin.

"After questions from the studio audience for thirty minutes, you will have an opportunity to sum up. The one who speaks first will get the last word. Normal rules of debate will apply. Speakers will not interrupt each other."

Garcia was thrown by getting everything he had wanted in the plans for this debate. He had no desire to win the election. When Miranda was dead, the country would need a strong man to lead it. He was a strong man. That was the main purpose of the debate in his mind — to show himself as strong and uncompromising on every issue.

He continued the discussion of details and of course insisted on getting Delia to produce a written summary which they could then both sign. His heart was not in this discussion. His thoughts were elsewhere.

He visualised making Miranda beg for mercy before he killed her and he smiled. Delia thought how different he looked when he smiled.

He came into Delia's office while she was typing up the agreement. He made her coffee and chatted amiably. So much so that when he asked her if she wanted to go for a drink after work she only hesitated for a moment before agreeing.

In recent months, Garcia always found it convenient to carry a little capsule in his pocket. He was toying with it while he spoke to Delia. It was called Rohypnol, or the date rape drug. Delia was in for a night to remember – if, that is, she remembered anything at all. He smiled that winning smile again at the thought and Delia saw the smile and reflected what a nice (and potentially both rich and powerful) man Garcia was.

The bar was busy. The Miranda bonuses were putting a smile on the faces of the brewers and innkeepers if nothing else.

"Did you ever think you would be working so closely with Miranda?"

"Should I be talking to you about Miranda? Aren't you her opponent?" Delia's smile belied her words. In any case, her capacity for gossip meant that Garcia just had to listen for a while to find out everything she knew.

"I am also the reason she is alive, the reason she is in power and the reason The Dictator is dead. Opponents perhaps but I hope we can be civilised about this. What are you drinking?"

"A bloody Mary for me." Delia replied promptly. She thought diluting the vodka would be a more cultured way to drink it.

Garcia was delighted. A bloody Mary was ideal for diluting Rohypnol. He knew to his cost that its presence would show up in gin and tonic by changing the colour. On the occasion on which that happened, he had angrily summoned the bartender and demanded another drink for his companion. He had had to rely on the traditional expedient of getting her blind drunk, a project she was quite happy to go along with.

He smiled winningly and ordered bloody Marys for the two of them. They retired to a corner table such as lovers might choose. He estimated that the third bloody Mary would be the one to slip the Rohypnol into. He wanted a bit of coherent conversation with Delia before she became incapable of it.

"She is a wonderful woman, you must be proud to be working so closely with her."

"Well I don't know about that, it is really my boss who is working closely with her on media issues. Still I do get to see her a lot and she calls me by name instead of 40D/487 which is a nice change.

"The hierarchy never knew the names of subordinates,

most of the time they wouldn't address us at all, by name or number. It was as if we weren't human. That is slowly changing.

"And Miranda is wonderful. The effort she has made for those poor street girls. They really are at the bottom of the heap socially and they have nobody to stand up for them. They prayed to Saint Miranda and, well it must seem like a miracle. Suddenly they are protected by the army instead of being screwed by them and being found jobs that don't involve opening their legs for disgusting old perverts."

"Does Miranda ever talk about her own past? Her relationship with the young Dictator for instance?"

"Let's have another drink, I'll tell you all about it."

Garcia obliged and Delia began in a confidential whisper.

"There is something you don't know. Miranda does not talk much about her past, not to me anyway. I know for a fact that the young Dictator is not her child. Wait. There's more.

"You seem to have downed that one quickly. I am having a job keeping up with you. I will get a couple more drinks."

Garcia put the drinks down on the way back to the table. His practice with the capsules had made him perfect. It was a matter of seconds to empty the capsule into the bloody Mary. The tomato juice was a perfect cover for the colour and the Worcester sauce helped to disguise the taste. It was ideal. Garcia made a mental note to cultivate women who drank bloody Marys in future.

Garcia listened as Delia told him the story he already knew about the Mirandas and The Dictator's children. He watched carefully to see her co-ordination and concentration deteriorate. He thought about what he was going to do to this woman soon and the familiar excitement grew.

The time came when she got up to go to the toilet. Suddenly she found that she just couldn't put one foot in front of the other accurately. She was momentarily frightened, but there was Garcia by her side following his practised routine. He was laughing to make her laugh, jollying her along, supporting her in her attempts to walk and gently mocking her attempts to talk. His attitude made the other people in the bar see her as a drunken woman and him as the good friend who was getting a taxi to get her home. He seldom drank in the same bar twice. He had a good working knowledge of the bars in the centre of the city by now.

The taxis were suffering from the changeover from control by the gangs. They were not being used as mobile brothels any more and had to find other fares. The gang-member drivers were usually quite good at finding their way around the city. The new men (and a few women) were relying on Satnavs.

Garcia had taken the precaution of finding out Delia's address from Human Resources because she was most certainly in no fit state to give it to anyone now. Delia was in a dreamlike state or perhaps more accurately a nightmare. The only good thing about it was her very good friend Garcia who was looking after her. Everything else was strange, so strange.

Garcia took her handbag and found her house-key because there was no chance of her finding the keyhole. He kissed her and put his hand inside her blouse in the taxi. She struggled ineffectually and he laughed affectionately. She laughed too. She was not entirely sure why she was laughing but once she started there seemed to be no reason to stop. She went on laughing and Garcia went on exploring under her clothes until she was quite out of breath.

Taxi drivers get to see a lot of things if they bother to look in the mirror. They get to hear a lot of things too. A groping man and a giggling woman scarcely raised an eyebrow, so long as the fare was paid in full. Garcia was scrupulously honest about paying taxi drivers and he was a generous tipper, now he had the money. Neeta and Petra had no further use for their wealth so Garcia had just appropriated it.

He used to joke, silently and privately, that he believed in the liberation of the working classes, one by one, starting with himself.

He arrived at Delia's house and unlocked the front door. He assisted her, she needed a lot of assistance, through the front door. She laughed when she walked into the table and upset the flower vase. He decided to dispense with the preliminaries, much as he liked the preliminaries, and to take her straight up the stairs. At least she moved as straight as she was capable. This was not very straight, in the event.

Miranda's office

Without his ADC, the under-secretary had to call on Miranda on person.

"Miranda," He still thrilled at the fact that he, a fairly lowly under-secretary, could address what he thought of as the head of state by her first name.

"I have received some disturbing reports from security services about the other candidate in the forthcoming election."

"Well he is a mass murderer, as we found out at the time of the St Michael's massacre. He forced Neeta and Petra to confess to all his crimes. He is planning to murder me. Is there anything I have missed out?"

"It seems, Miranda, that he is a serial rapist." He was pleased to have a piece of information which she was not privy to.

"You have evidence?"

" Firstly there is one woman who he was seen with in a bar in town. She drank with him but after only three drinks she was seriously incapacitated, He made a clumsy attempt to appear to be a friend who was trying to get her out of the bar without her coming to grief. She went with him in a taxi and she has no recollection of what happened to her. However the medical reports show that she had traces of a drug called Rohypnol. It is called a..."

"I am familiar with it."

"Well she also had signs of recent violent sexual activity. This led the security services to keep a close eye on Garcia."

"I instructed them to keep a close eye on Garcia, but please continue."

"The second victim was much the same. The other people in the bar noted that Garcia was obviously very fond of her and helping her to get home safely after a tough night. She had evidence of extreme sexual violence both in terms of... do you need the details?"

"Skip it for now, but your thoroughness is noted."

"The third victim had no traces of Rohypnol but a barkeeper noticed that he returned a drink for no particular reason. The victim was a hard drinker who knew exactly what the ' disgusting little pervert' as she called him had got up to with her and she has made a full statement."

"The fourth victim..." He hesitated.

"What is it?"

"I came to you so late because it seems that the next victim might turn out to be Delia 40D/487"

"For the last time, stop calling her that. I know Delia. I even know a little of her story but she has a lot more to say. Are you saying that he has raped Delia?"

"I am saying that he left a bar with her ninety minutes ago and I came to you as soon as I knew this fact."

"I cannot sit here. I know security can handle this but perhaps I can emphasise the importance. You come with me. Bring six of my security men, you know the ones I mean. I don't care how it looks for me to be involved in a security operation. I think of it as helping a friend in trouble.

"Please understand this. I want him caught alive and brought to trial. If I can avenge Delia and the other women, it will be worth it."

The under-secretary kept to himself the thought that it would be very good political propaganda. After all Miranda already knew all about that.

Lucy and Delia

Garcia knew perfectly well that Delia lived alone. She had said so and her service record confirmed it. She had never told anyone about Lucy while Lucy was in danger from the street gangs and in any case it was nobody else's business.

Her room was the first door you came to at the top of the stairs. She had still been giggling on her clumsy stumbling progress up the staircase. Garcia kicked the door open and threw Delia on to the bed. He ripped off her blouse and her bra. She made a feeble effort to stop him ripping off her skirt and knickers. Garcia laughed cruelly as he easily pushed her hands away. She was not giggling now.

Delia started to cry out. Garcia was ready for this and he stuffed her mouth with her knickers. He tied the gag in place with a stocking. She was fighting for breath. Garcia had a taste for the most brutal sex since his training by Neeta and Petra.

It was as if his mind was in two parts. There was his liking for Delia and his enjoyment of her company and that was genuine enough. And then on the other hand, there was his excitement at domination and cruelty. And at the moment that excitement controlled all his actions.

He promised himself that he would be as nice as pie to Delia in the morning so that she would find it hard to believe in the "other" Garcia of the night before. If she remembered anything at all, she would think of the whole thing as a bad dream.

He imagined the conversation which they would have, "You got a bit drunk last night, Delia. I brought you home in a taxi and then when you came through the front door you walked right into the table. Just have a look at the bruises. You poor thing."

Suddenly, Garcia noticed that Delia had stopped struggling. For him the resistance of a helpless victim was part of the entertainment. She had stopped moving altogether. Her chest wasn't moving, she had stopped breathing altogether. Garcia had plenty of witnesses that he had gone home with her. He couldn't just run, although that was a temptation. He needed to think. He blundered his way through the unfamiliar house to the bathroom and splashed cold water on his face.

Lucy was tossing in an uncomfortable dream about her old life on the street. She was trying to get away from a particularly vicious client but the car doors were locked. She was hammering uselessly on the toughened glass. Something woke her up. Was that a bloody elephant in the bathroom making all that noise? She ran straight to her mother.

Her mother was stretched naked on the bed. Ripped clothes were strewn around the room. Lucy didn't stop to think what that might mean. Here was her mother and she needed her right away.

She took Delia by the shoulder.

"Wake up mum, for Christ's sake wake up. There is somebody in the house. We have to get out. You must wake up!"

She shook harder. Her mother was not breathing! She wasn't going to wake up, ever. Whoever had ripped her clothes had killed her. AND HE WAS STILL IN THE BLOODY HOUSE!

Lucy had no other thought than escape as she ran blindly out of the room. She was distracted by a booming sound from downstairs and she ran straight into Garcia coming back up the stairs. He made a grab for her and she put all her weight behind her fists. The big man overbalanced and tumbled down the stairs.

His head hit the concrete floor with a sickening crunch and blood started to spread from the wound in the back of his head. He moved like a man having a seizure and Lucy watched fascinated as he lay still and the blood spread from wall to wall.

There was one final "boom" and the front door gave way to the battering. Armed men started streaming in. Lucy was paralysed with fear. The men stepped over Garcia. One of them stood over the body with a quite unnecessary machine gun trained on the corpse with the shattered skull. It was something to do.

Two others pointed their guns at Lucy. "Where is Delia?"

Lucy gestured dumbly to the door of the room upstairs and one man raced up.

Another kept his gun pointed at Lucy.

"And who the fuck are you?"

"Who the fuck are you? This is my house. It's the middle of the night and you come in without so much as a 'by-your-leave'."

"Listen you stupid little tart..." was as far as he got.

It was like a dream to Lucy. Suddenly Miranda was there. Miranda was standing in her house. She was giving the man a good talking-to. "We need to find out who this girl is but you will not treat her with disrespect in my presence. And I suggest you don't do it when you are not in my presence."

The man in Delia's room interrupted the lecture by calling

down the stairs. "We need an ambulance. Quick."

Miranda raced up the stairs. She looked at Delia lying on the bed. She put her hand behind her head.

"We are too late, she is dead." The secret service man was not a medical expert.

Miranda was a medical expert, or to be precise she was a mother which comes to the same thing. She held Delia's nose and breathed into her mouth. She watched her chest fall and repeated the breath. The secret service were trained in all sorts of things, most of which you really don't want to know about, but they had never seen this before.

Eventually, Delia gave a choking sound and drew in breath noisily. The ambulance crew arrived and took her away. She was, they said, out of danger.

"Miranda brought a woman back from the dead" was the story which ran like wildfire through the City. It did not do her saintly reputation any harm.

Darijus Dagys organised a press conference. In it, the story of Miranda bringing Delia back from the dead was explicitly denied. Did that stop the rumours? No of course not.

The tragic and accidental death of Garcia raised a lot of questions. Reporters in The Dictatorship were just getting into the habit of actually asking questions rather than waiting to be given the answers.

Darijus was practised in the tactic of giving the same answer several times until the reporters realised that was all the answer they were going to get.

"Delia and Garcia were very good friends and all the evidence indicates that he was rushing to get medical assistance when he tripped and fell."

"Were Miranda and the security men on the premises at the time?"

"No. We have video evidence of their arrival after the tragic accident."

"Is it true that Miranda is holding talks with the Revolutionary Party?" One of the new breed of female journalists asked that question.

"Miranda is a servant of the people. The Revolutionary Party is now a legal organisation and the ban on their radio station has been lifted as of this morning. They are engaged in talks with Miranda's advisers."

"Is it true that the election has been cancelled?"

"The election will go ahead but voters will have the option of voting for or against Miranda. By law all elections from now on will have "None of the above" as an option on the ballot paper. If the voters reject Miranda, there will be fresh elections.

"Long live Miranda!"

Darijus stood up to deliver the last sentence. It was echoed by all the civil servants in the room and the journalists felt they had to join in, so they did. The female journalist was the first to her feet.

The Revolutionary Party

Later that day, Darijus had another meeting with the Revolutionary Party and a debriefing for Miranda afterwards. The fiction that it was 'her advisers' who were talking to the Revolutionary Party had to be maintained, Darijus insisted, but it only slowed matters up slightly.

Xavier, Wolfie and Sister Lam were present. The Revolutionary Party had a list of demands. They would not support Miranda but they would publicise those parts of her program which they supported. This was described as "a fig leaf" by Darijus. They dare not support Miranda because it would compromise their revolutionary credentials. They dare not oppose Miranda because, even in their own ranks, she was the most popular conceivable candidate for leadership.

The Revolutionary Party demanded that their radio station should be unbanned. That had already taken place. They wanted free trade unions, Miranda did too. They wanted freedom of speech.

Miranda laughed. "Well for heaven's sake. 'Freedom of speech' is such a vague concept that anyone could agree to it. There are no laws on libel or slander. The newspapers can publish what they like. That has always been the case. It is just that if what they liked wasn't what The Dictator liked then the journalist would disappear as if by magic."

"These demands are ridiculously modest," Xavier chipped in. "There is no nationalisation of the land, no expropriation of the rich, not even one banker strung up from a lamp-post. What sort of revolutionaries are they?"

"I asked them the same question," Darijus responded soberly, "What they said was ahem they said they er um didn't want to sow illusions in Miranda."

When they heard this, Wolfie and Xavier looked each other in the eye and just burst out laughing. Miranda eventually called them to order but there were tears of laughter running down her face.

"According to you, and I have no reason to doubt what you told me, these bastards sat down and negotiated with Garcia. They knew full well he intended to assassinate me and it didn't occur to them to inform me. Now they are worried about sowing illusions. And the Revolutionary Committee?

"They are being liquidated. Sorry I mean by that, the organisation is being liquidated and they are joining the Revolutionary Party. Some of them are forming a "followers of St Miranda" group – a non-segregated version of the Sisters of Miranda. They hope to attract people from the Revolutionary Party.

"I also have news of Delia. She will be out of hospital today and she wants to come back to work tomorrow."

"Well thank God for that."

"Well the election seems safe– one should never predict these things – but then it will be time for us to disappear." Sister Lam explained.

"What literally?" Miranda asked. Darijus was on the verge of laughing when he saw that Miranda was actually asking a serious question.

The trio remained silent. "Actually on second thoughts it is best that I don't know too much." Miranda concluded..

Victory for Miranda

The trio sat at the back of the Church of Saint Miranda. The service had concluded and a screen had been rolled down over the Eastern window on which a live TV feed was being broadcast. The followers of Miranda had been welcomed, maybe not with open arms but welcomed, by the Sisterhood.

As the election results came in, excited crowds from across the country filled the screen. There was colour and music and singing. There was prayer ("and thankfully no speeches," Wolfie remarked.) As the final result, a ringing endorsement of Miranda, was announced, the congregation rose as one; "Long live Saint Miranda!" There was hope and confidence in the way they stood. There were tears in their eyes.

They didn't notice three members of the congregation had literally vanished from the back row.

The End

Appendix One

Wolf-Dietrich Von Raitenau is a real character. The idea which set me off on writing *Salt Wars* and *The Miranda Revolution* was this: although I cannot travel in time because of the paradoxes it would create, in dreams we can go anywhere and to any time. So if I dreamed of having a conversation with Wolf-Dietrich Von Raitenau, who died 400 years ago, and Wolf-Dietrich dreamed about talking to someone from the future and *it was the same conversation* then the impossibility of time travel was overcome, from a certain point of view.

I had the putative conversation in the graveyard of St Sebastian where a tour guide had explained that Wolf-Dietrich would have wanted a simple burial and not the tasteless mausoleum which was built there. I do not know if this is true.

Stories multiply around Wolf-Dietrich Von Raitenau. In many ways he was a child prodigy. At the age of only 11 he was appointed canon of the Cathedral in Constance. Having relatives in the highest councils of the Catholic Church probably did him no harm.

He studied at the German College in Rome before taking his post as a canon in the Cathedral of Salzburg. He was 19 years old. He was only 28 when he took over the immensely powerful role of Prince-Archbishop of Salzburg.

All the stories about Wolf-Dietrich say that he would have

preferred a military career. When he became Archbishop (and therefore ruler) of Salzburg, he was in a position to pursue the most unwise military action of his life. He invaded the Berchtesgaden Provostry, which was also claimed by the Bavarian House of Wittelsbach. In the subsequent fighting, Wolf-Dietrich was captured while seeking to escape to Carinthia. He was deposed and imprisoned for life by his nephew and successor Markus Sittikus von Hohenems. It is unlikely that he felt very avuncular towards the little so-and-so.

His motive throughout however was to keep Salzburg independent of both Austria and Bavaria. The economic foundation of this independence was Salzburg salt which is still mined to this day. He even brought in a law in 1606 known as the "Eternal Statute" which forbade any prince of Austria or Bavaria becoming the Archbishop of Salzburg. However, only God is eternal and Salzburg is now incorporated into Austria.

The building known today as the Mirabell Palace (which was used in the film *The Sound of Music*) was actually built for Wolf-Dietrich's mistress Salome Alt, with whom he had fifteen children. He had applied for permission to marry but it never came through. The post was awful in those days.

At the beginning of his reign he continued the policies of his day, expelling non-Catholics from Salzburg. I have seen the same intolerance displayed in Amsterdam where I visited a church which was hidden from the world in a private house while all the Catholic churches were appropriated by the

Protestants. Historians claim that Wolf-Dietrich mellowed later in his reign, although his refusal to join the Catholic League probably had more to do with preserving the independence of Salzburg than with any opposition to their objectives.

All conversations with him would of course have to be conducted in Latin. Latin is to this day the language of the church. As a Catholic (universal) Church it preserves the use of a dead language and adapts it to make communication possible. I have translated the conversations into the vernacular for the benefit of readers!

The Church holds mass in the vernacular these days and the form of the mass would seem strange to Wolf-Dietrich. There is much more involvement of the laity in the ceremony and the priest normally faces the congregation. In the Tridentine mass, the priest would have his back to the congregation because he was offering mass on their behalf. The Latin mass is quite difficult to understand even if you are familiar with the language. It is not likely that a large number of the peasantry were familiar with the language so the change, brought about in the wake of the second Vatican council was widely (though not universally) welcomed as making the mass more accessible to the people.

Wolf-Dietrich was an adaptable soul although some things, like the independence of Salzburg, were non-negotiable in his mind. He would have come to terms with celebrating the modern mass eventually. In the present day he would be a priest although not holding the rank of Archbishop.

Very little is known about the children of Wolf-Dietrich, save the fact that they indicate that his relationship with Salome Alt was a long-lasting one. When he was imprisoned, she was banished to Wels, Austria in Stadtplatz, where she and the children went to live. It is generally thought that there were no surviving grandchildren but like everything else about Wolf-Dietrich there is history and there is legend. It is possible at a time when Europe was devastated and disrupted by plague that the records of any grandchildren were lost and that they would seek to remain incognito. Wolf-Dietrich would have had many enemies in Austria and Germany. People with the surname Reitnawer might or might not be descendants of Wolf-Dietrich. They might have wanted to disown him at the time but their descendants today would be happier to claim him as an illustrious ancestor.

Salome Alt was the daughter of the merchant and city Councillor Wilhelm Alt of Salzburg and the granddaughter of Ludwig Alt, mayor of Salzburg. She is said to have met Wolf-Dietrich at a party. To be the mistress of the Prince-Archbishop was a substantial step up the social ladder. After the death of Wolf-Dietrich in 1617, she is said to have dressed in mourning like a widow for the rest of her life. If so it was a sign of the great love between them. It was said of her that "she had no enemies." If so, she was quite different from Wolf-Dietrich in that respect.

Characters

The Dictator
The Dictator has no name. His father did but nobody was permitted to use it. He made sure his son was only ever called "The Dictator's son". There was no question of his daughters being allowed to inherit and no question of more than one son surviving.

Xavier Hollands
Torturer to Wolf-Dietrich with an aversion to actually torturing anyone but mental powers which compensate for this.

Tilly Hollands
(nee Brandwine) Wife of Xavier. Her name really is 'Tilly'. It is not short for Matilda. See also Sister Lam.

Wolf-Dietrich Von Raitenau
Prince-Archbishop of Salzburg. Somehow he gets roped in to Xavier's battle with The Dictator. See Appendix 1.

Kaspar
Reporter who turns up in Ye Olde Boar with an amazing tale about The Dictator. There is more to him than meets the eye.

Neeta and Petra
The Dictator's twins. Possibly the Devil's. Petra has a deeper voice. This is important as they are otherwise very hard to tell apart. They have been brought up to torture and kill without mercy.

Will
Rebel #1 – a member of the Revolutionary Committee.

Garcia
Rebel #2. Garcia is an intelligent and very attractive young man as he would be the first to tell you.

Karl
Rebel #3. He was named after Karl Marx. A bold move by his parents who never told anybody and claimed it was an "Uncle Karl" he was named after.

Ygael
Rebel #4. Ygael is the Chairman of the Revolutionary Committee at the time the story opens.

Father Simon
The Priest of St Michael's Church. Quite a contrast to Wolf-Dietrich as a man of God.

Marcos
The man with the car and pimp to Sarah.

Sarah
A bone-thin street girl. Marcos is her pimp.

Sister Lam
The persona Tilly chose to adopt in the Dictatorship.

Geert Hollands
Adoptive Mother of Xavier. Her greatest wish was to meet a well-manicured young man she could take as a lover. Be careful what you wish for!

Terrance Hollands
Father of Xavier, former ICI employee and scientist.

Mitch
Pimp#1.

The Man
Pimp#2 and uncle of uncles. Real name Cedric.

Doctor
Pimp#3 real name Phil.

Shelly/Sheila/Suki
Under-age Girl#1 Mitch's girl.

Delia/Lucy/
Under-age Girl#2 one of The Man's girls.

Maria/Jenny
Under-age Girl #3 The Doctor's girl and daughter of Miranda.

Lucas
Street thug.

Connie
Girlfriend of Lucas.

Miranda
Consort of The Dictator. Although Miranda is worshipped as a saint, there are in fact many "Mirandas" at the time our story opens. One is the mother of Maria/Jenny.

Charles
Cousin of Father Alon and owner of the cafe where the street girls hang out when not working.

Father Alon
The priest of Saint Miranda's Church and cousin of Charles.

Captain Brand
Female "handler" of the satanic twins. She is a tall dark-haired woman in her mid forties.

Quin
Jailer and torturer. A pupil of Captain Brand.

Lynda or occasionally Morganna
The Doctor's replacement for Jenny.

Darijus Dagys
Under-secretary for communications

Sergeant Marach
One of the soldiers who side with Miranda.

Sergeant Michael
One of the soldiers who works with Sister Lam.

Commander Nelson
Head of security assigned to deal with the street gangs under The Dictatorship.

The Boss
Leading gangster in the capital city – has information with which to blackmail anybody and everybody.

Soldiers
A whole cast of ordinary soldiers who find themselves doing extraordinary things for Saint Miranda.

About the Writer, Derek McMillan

I live in Durrington-on-Sea in Sussex with my wife, Angela, who is also my editor. We both love reading books and watching TV together, often detective stories such as Broadchurch. We also enjoy the soaps EastEnders and Coronation Street. There are so many story lines that at any one time there is usually one which is controversial, emotionally engaging or intriguing.

I have always been a fan of Science Fiction and I think the Mirror of Eternity stories (which are all available on Kindle) show this. I have also written flash fiction for Everydayfiction.com, Saturdaynightreader.com and

Alfiedog.com

Printed in Great Britain
by Amazon